THE CODE SNATCH

THE CODE SNATCH

ALAN STRIPP

This edition published in 2013 by:
Thistle Publishing
36 Great Smith Street
London
SW1P 3BU

ISBN-13: 978-1-909869-75-2

FOREWORD
By Nigel West

O n one point historians are agreed: the extraordinary contribution made by Allied cryptanalysts during the Second
World War had a significant impact on the successful prosecution
of the conflict, and shortened it by up to two years. This remarkable achievement was accomplished by imaginative electrical engineers, brilliant cryptanalysts, inspired linguists who were brought
together in what was probably the greatest concentration of intel-
lectual power ever gathered for a single purpose. While it might
be argued that some of the world's greatest physicists and chemists
were recruited into the Manhattan Project to develop the atomic
bomb, supported by an unprecedented industrial investment, the
cryptographers assembled by the Anglo-American code-breakers
combined many disciplines to solve a wide variety of enemy ciphers,
among them hand-ciphers, machine-generated ciphers and even
the notoriously challenging one-time pads. That success would have
a lasting impact into the Cold War as the techniques created for
application against the Axis would find other targets in the Soviet
Bloc.

In his Author's Note in *The Code Snatch* Alan Stripp strongly
implies, but does not assert outright, that his novel was based on an
'unusual, colourful and successful operation' in which he partici-
pated in late 1944 as part of an effort in Mingaladen in Burma to
obtain a Japanese codebook.

Although plenty of highly imaginative schemes were proposed
to provide short-cuts or 'cribs' to ease the cryptographers' task.
However, there was a predisposition to avoid outright theft where

it was likely that the loss would be detected, and it could be anticipated that the enemy would take the appropriate counter-measures to mitigate the damage. In one case a pair of over-enthusiastic member of the U.S. Office of Strategic Services were prevented at the very last moment from carrying out a planned burglary on the Japanese naval attaché's office in Lisbon. Their objective was to steal a diplomatic code, apparently unaware that the system had been solved already, and their intervention would prove wholly counter-productive and probably result in terminating a valuable source of Allied intelligence. Similarly, an elaborate but ill-judged proposal, Operation RUTHLESS made by Lieutenant-Commander Ian Fleming in October 1940 to seize a cipher machine from a German rescue vessel was scrapped for much the same reason. The likely consequence would have been a tightening of the enemy's security procedures, and maybe even a complete change in their systems.

In the light of the obvious hazards intrinsic in such high-risk snatches, one is bound to wonder whether Stripp's tale is rather more of a self-indulgent conceit rather than a veiled version of the truth, allegedly crafted deliberately to circumvent the Ministry of Defence's strictures. On the face of it, anything that placed personnel with a knowledge of future plans or intelligence sources and methods was subject to a ban that, quite sensibly, was rigorously enforced upon pain of a summary court-martial. Sripp's account appears to breach the prohibition, but would the author have placed his impressive reputation by perpetrating what amounts to a hoax? His memorial service, held in 2009, was attended by many friends, admirers, former pupils and senior members of the intelligence community, a sign of the high regard in which he was held by his fellow professionals. Might he have deliberately placed his standing in such jeopardy?

The reality is that only a small proportion of what might be termed the Second World War's intelligence dimension has been revealed. Little has been disclosed, for example, about Japan's cipher bureau, the Tokushu Joho Bu, or even the German equivalent, the

Oberkommando des Heeres, General der Nachrichten Aufklarung, (abbreviated OKIi/GdNA) located at Jueterbog, which employed a staff of more than 60,000. There is much to be researched and published, even among the documents that have been declassified already, so perhaps there are further surprises for us in the near future.

Author's Note

In order to soothe the sensibilities of the Ministry of Defence, who still keep an eagle eye on things that happened in World War Two, I have taken liberties with some of the technical details of this unusual, colourful and successful operation, and with the identities of those involved in it.

Nevertheless I hope that this book will fill a gap in the history of secret intelligence in the war of 1939-1945.

A.S.

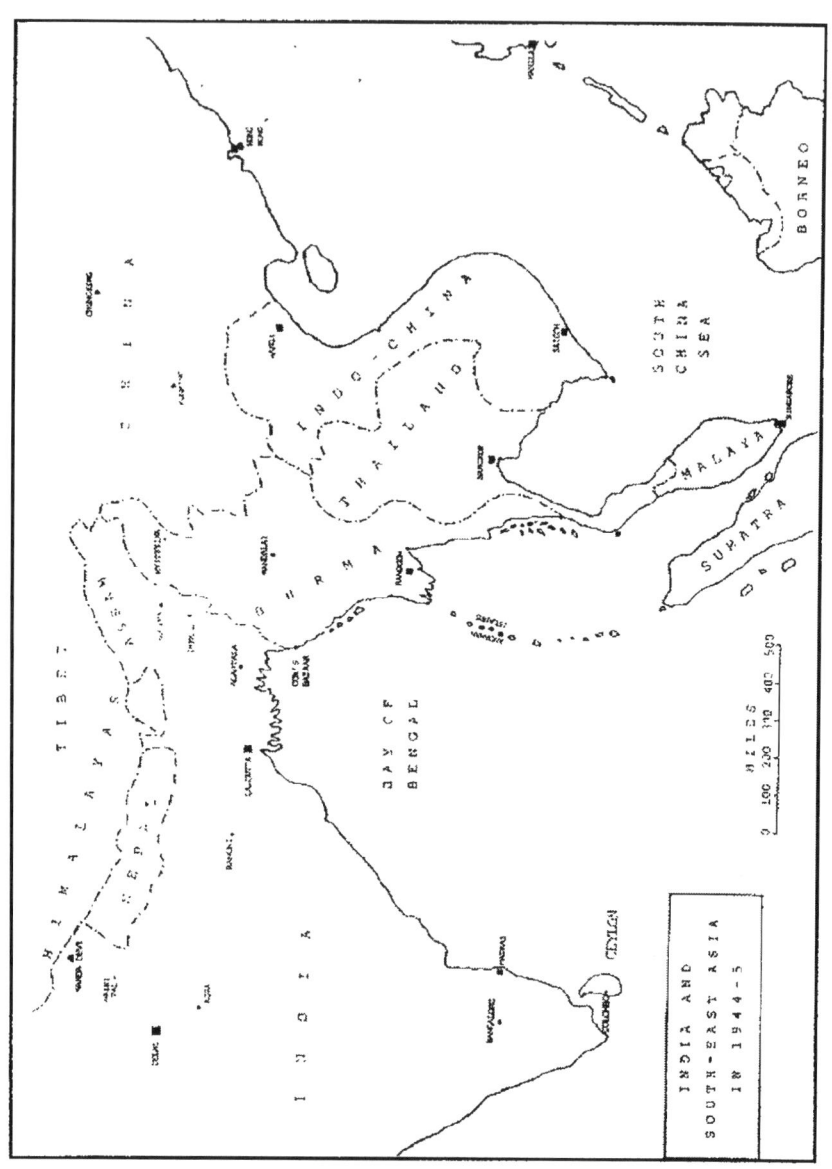

INDIA AND SOUTH-EAST ASIA

CONTENTS

PROLOGUE

It was kind of the General to come and see us off. The scheme had not been his brainchild, but he had liked it from the start and backed it against the sceptics. Thanks to him, what began as a madcap idea had grown into a workable plan. In the end the military hierarchy, from Mountbatten – an enthusiast for new ideas, dotty or sane – down to some fairly stolid staff officers, had given it their blessing and support.

There had been plenty of raised eyebrows. Nobody disputed the urgent need to stop the Japanese from bringing their new codebook into use. We had to keep open the flow of vital information we were getting from the current book – but how? The ingenuity, the sheer beauty of this operation, was that the enemy were going to *give* us their new codebook. That at least is what we hoped. We wouldn't know for certain until a few hours later, and that uncertainty, coupled with the knowledge that if our bluff were called it would be a suicide mission, meant that all of us had to be volunteers.

Meanwhile, here we were, five Allied officers climbing into a captured Japanese bomber one muggy morning, not far from Calcutta. An unlikely story? I agree. To explain, I must go back to the beginning.

It all began at General Slim's headquarters.

Slim, the British commander of the Fourteenth Army in Burma, had a lot to think about in late 1944. His troops had crushed the fanatical Japanese assault on Assam and proved that the enemy were not supermen. He needed to push them back and keep them on the trot, and he knew he could win that round.

But in the next round he needed a knockout blow. If he merely pushed them further south, his supply lines, across some of the worst mountains and jungles in the world, would be stretched to the limit, while the enemy would draw closer to their reserves of men and supplies all the time. He also had to contend with some of the worst weather in the world; in early May the monsoon would arrive, drowning the flatter parts of Burma and converting the precipitous mountain slopes into liquid mud. And then the war would last a year longer.

To defeat the Japanese decisively Slim had to know where they were going to stand and fight. He needed to know it urgently, otherwise he might lose his slender margin of superiority and throw away this chance of victory.

This is where we came in. There are various ways of finding out what the enemy is up to, but one way beats all the rest: breaking their codes. My unit in Delhi, cover-named the Wireless Experimental Centre, looked after our codebreaking in south-east Asia, and for some time we had been supplying General Slim with just the details he wanted. So he told us that he liked the stuff we were sending him, hinted discreetly that he would shortly be making some crucial decisions, and told us to focus even more sharply on what his opposite number, General Kimura, was planning in central Burma.

Unfortunately this came at a very bad moment. We had learned from signals broken a few days earlier that the codebook for the Japanese Army Air Force, our valued and productive friend 2244, was about to be changed. As soon as that happened, a curtain would descend and cut off the whole picture – until we could break the new book, which might take months. We had already been racking our brains about this, but Slim's message startled us into realising the full implications. The hope of speedy and complete victory in Burma might be jeopardised and the enemy might even be able to regain the initiative. Moreover, if the campaign dragged on for another year because it could not be clinched before the monsoon, then tens of thousands more soldiers and airmen might be killed, to say nothing of the countless prisoners the Japanese were holding, often in barbarous conditions.

We gathered that General Slim took this blow remarkably well. This was hardly surprising, after all the disasters he had survived in the evacuation of Burma. He had said at one stage, "If someone brings me a piece of good news I shall burst into tears," and later added laconically, "I was never put to the test." So he simply thrust his pugnacious lower lip further forward and borrowed Wavell's ominous phrase: "I see."

He sent us another message. "I want you all to think very hard. Anybody with a proposal for getting round this will have it properly discussed. No pouring of cold water merely because it's unorthodox. I'm sending you one of my best staff officers to help. You know how urgent this is. One of you may be able to lay the golden egg. Good luck – and get a move on."

Day One:
Preston Takes The Chair

I suppose it was inevitable that when our meeting started, those with pet schemes would take the floor; the grinding of well-worn axes mingled with the neighing of familiar hobby-horses. We were soon joined by a couple of colonels, the senior of whom indicated that he wanted us to carry on. He listened attentively and waited till we ran out of steam before he took over.

"Gentlemen, I'm grateful to you for starting the ball rolling. My name is Preston and this is Lieutenant-Colonel Agnew. The General has sent me to deputise for him. I want you to keep meeting as long and as often as seems profitable, and I shall sit in on all your discussions – night shifts included. If anyone has a suggestion to put to me personally, because he thinks it might be howled down in public, he will be welcome. I stress that we are open to all ideas that stand any chance of success, however farfetched, and regardless of rank. If you want my help in any way, let me know."

He was a friendly man, with natural authority and a crisp but genial manner; tall and sturdily built, with piercing blue eyes and an aquiline nose. I suppose he was in his early fifties. Agnew was smaller, well groomed, with a quick-darting glance and a prim smile. He seemed to be only half listening to Preston – a semi-detached man. Preston continued, "Before we go further I want to hear more about the intelligence this Army Air Force code provides – 2244, you call it? What is so special about it?"

This was my province, so I explained. Aerial reconnaissance, spies, captured documents and interrogated prisoners can all

1

supply titbits of information but rarely provide an overall picture. Breaking an enemy's codes can, because they penetrate to his innermost thoughts and plans. Even routine reports on casualties, ration returns and petrol stocks can show if a division is vulnerable or in good shape. It is like hearing the enemy commander talking to himself – round the clock.

The Army Air Force code system 2244 told us how many planes the Japs had, where they were based, how many were serviceable, what stocks of fuel and ammunition they had, and how many aircrew were available. Sometimes it also revealed their future plans. In a country of mountains, swamps and jungles like Burma, aircraft can fly only from a few airfields, so every time a squadron was ordered to move from X to Y it helped to show the enemy's intentions. Most Japanese warships were back in the Pacific, trying to contain the Americans' island-hopping, so there weren't many naval signals to help us.

"But what about the Jap army stuff? There seem to be plenty of them about."

"Sir, neither we nor the Yanks have made any real headway breaking it. That's why 2244's our best ally."

I added that we felt sure that any new 2244 codebook could be broken. After all, we had broken the current one, and when the Americans later picked up a copy in the Solomon Islands there were no discrepancies to speak of. But breaking it had taken us a year. That would be no use to Slim. Even a one-month delay could mean his being disastrously wrong-footed in central Burma.

"Fair enough," Preston conceded. "Now let me tell you about the military options. We've looked at cutting-out operations – smash-and-grab if you prefer – and we don't fancy our chances. We doubt if our forward troops could capture the new book at an enemy air-field. They might well storm the place, but they've only an outside chance of finding the signals office *and* pinching the right book before the Japs destroy it. Paratroops? Practically none in our the-atre; as usual we're the poor relations. Commandos? Same answer; there aren't any. Glider-borne troops? Wingate used them in the second Chindit affair; they are all right landing in isolated clearings, but near an airfield they'd be mincemeat. We don't believe that any of these ideas would work. You agree, Agnew?"

Agnew gave a wintry smile that didn't reach his eyes. "I think that is a fair assessment, Colonel. An orthodox operation, such as many of us might prefer, would be difficult to mount and we could not guarantee its success." He spoke clearly but pedantically, like a lawyer reading a will: an authentic Dryasdust. "I am not sure, however, that an unorthodox one would fare any better."

"Very well," Preston went on. "You all know that the reason for urgency is the monsoon, but you may not realise what a stranglehold that has on our logistics. In Burma the flat parts get flooded a yard or more deep. That's child's play compared to the mountains where we are trying to get our tanks and trucks forward. There's one spot we call Chocolate Staircase. The track climbs over 3,000 feet – that's the height of Snowdon – in ten miles, with forty hairpin bends. In the monsoon it vanishes every few days. There's a bloody great rumbling noise and an avalanche wipes it off the map again. Don't run away with the idea that it's a minor road for us. Even an Irish farmer would hardly recognise it as a cart track, but that's our main supply route. There's no way round. So that's another reason why we've got to get to Rangoon before the monsoon does."

He then quoted the remark made by one of the Fourteenth Army engineers: "'The difficult can be done at once; the impossible may take a bit longer,'" and went on, "If, as we seem to agree," and he shot a glance at Agnew, "the orthodox ideas won't work, let's move on to the more fanciful ones. I'll hand over to you."

Eckersley jumped in. "What about a cloak-and-dagger job to steal the codebook, sir, if a military operation is out? Just to borrow it? Photograph it overnight, put it back next morning. Then they'd never know we'd had it."

A chorus of voices pointed out that he'd been reading too many spy thrillers, and anyway, he'd forgotten that a signals HQ would be open round the clock, just like us. Anyway, how could we get hold of it? In Europe it is just possible, with perfect command of a foreign language, to get into some security areas by disguise or sheer bluff. For a European to masquerade as a Japanese is virtually impossible …

My mind had been wandering ever since Preston had used the phrase 'I'll hand over to you.' Suddenly I knew what we had to do. Instead of stealing the new codebook, we had to coax the Japanese into handing it over to us!

The idea was simple to the point of absurdity. Nothing was likely to persuade them to do anything so silly. But supposing an order came from one of their own side? From one of their own higher command? A bogus order from us, put into the mouth of a high-ranking Japanese officer? Who? How? Where?

Another speaker was suggesting that we should try to pinpoint every enemy signals unit in Burma and then get the RAF to knock them out afresh every day, thus crippling their whole radio network. But others reminded him that we didn't want to stop their signals flowing; we needed to keep reading them. Besides, if this hare-brained scheme worked, they would still need to communicate somehow. If they went over to native runners and carrier pigeons, how could we intercept them? A gloomy and unidentifiable voice from the back of the room commented, "And we would all be out of a job."

Agnew frowned while a roar of laughter went up; Preston smiled tolerantly. "I don't think you will be on the dole queue yet. 'Satan finds some mischief still for idle hands to do.'" He looked at his watch. "Any more idle thoughts before we break for lunch?"

I plucked up courage and put my fantasy forward; I couldn't call it a suggestion. Friends who knew that I had a lively imagination smiled. They could see the logic, but how to apply it in practice? Preston and Agnew also seemed unimpressed. Nevertheless, when the meeting broke up, Preston beckoned me over. "Come and see me after lunch, Lieutenant Martyn. I think it's a non-starter, but it's worth looking at before we bury it."

He lunched with the directing staff, so I finished well before he did. I left the mess and walked in the quiet sultry haze trying to sort out my equally hazy thoughts. None of them seemed practicable, yet the idea itself still fascinated me. I went over to his room.

As I went in I noticed a Farsi dictionary open on his desk; so he was not just one of those 'simple soldier men' who work their way up to be safe, unimaginative staff officers in cushy jobs. We sat with a map of south-east Asia spread across a low table, and black coffee to keep us alert. The afternoon was sticky and it was all too easy to let our thoughts freewheel.

"Let's start from scratch. Assume for the sake of argument that we could get a bogus signal into their network, never mind how. How do we persuade them to hand over the new codebook to someone they don't know?"

"By exploiting their Bushido tradition – the unquestioning obedience to orders. If an order purported to come from high enough up, then a Major at an HQ signals unit – I think that's about the rank – wouldn't question it, especially if it were hedged about with all sorts of gipsy's warnings. You know, sir: the honour of the Emperor at stake, absolute secrecy vital, undeviating observance of instructions essential."

He gave a sudden boyish grin. "Let's hope you're right. How do we get the book out?"

That was my biggest headache. I presumed it would have to be flown out, but on what pretext, let alone in what aircraft, I could not begin to imagine.

"Never mind. Next question: what's the result going to be? The moment they realise we've got the book, surely they'll change again, so we'll be no better off."

"I doubt if they have another new book ready. It takes a long time to prepare one from scratch, and distributing it to units scattered all over the area takes a hell of a time. With any luck they couldn't complete that in time to spike the General's guns. The beauty of this scheme, though I say it myself, is that we've got them either way. If they don't find out that we've snatched the new book they'll go ahead and use it, and we can read it until further notice. If they do find out, they'll go back to the old one for as long as we need. Either way we've got them cold."

He stood up, stretched and padded to and fro across the worn Qashgai rug like a panther. "It's an attractive idea, Martyn, but how the dickens can we make it work? For example, how do we get the bogus message to our hypothetical Major?"

"That's a bit easier, sir. We use the current 2244 system and mimic their operator drill. To make it plausible we'd have to sneak in and send the signal from somewhere along the same bearing as a real Jap signals unit, in case they are doing direction-finding on us."

"Let's look at the map* , assuming we plan to snatch the book in Burma; I doubt if we could operate further afield than that."

It looked hopeless. Rangoon would be the best snatch-point equipped with the codebook, but the likeliest HQ to send them an order about handing it over would be Bangkok or Saigon – both at extreme aircraft range and with virtually no hope of help from the locals. Sumatra and Java were easier to reach, and there might be some hope of clandestine support on the ground, but neither had an HQ likely to transmit orders to Rangoon.

I said tentatively, "What about Singapore? What about our stay-behind men in Malaya? Could one of them send a bogus message as if it came from Southern Army HQ at Singapore?"

We looked at the map again. Forlorn as it was, that seemed our best hope.

"You'd better let me do some telephoning. Go and meditate on the signals and crypto implications. Think about the text of the message. And where the devil do we find a Jap aircraft?"

I went outside. It was cooler now, but a light breeze was whipping up gritty dust-devils in the sandy soil, so I went back to my room and tried to knock some sense into my ideas.

The bogus signal would have to purport to come from someone right outside Rangoon's normal orbit, with credentials that nobody

* see map on page 154

6

would dare to question. Even Southern Army HQ was hardly exalted enough. It must claim to originate from Imperial HQ in Tokyo, then heels would be clicked and no questions asked – but the bogus signal itself would still have to be sent from Malaya, in fact and in make-believe. The Japanese were known to use direction-finding sets to try to track down our undercover operators, so that if our signal were not sent from where it claimed, or very close, that would arouse their suspicions and jeopardise the whole plan – starting with the lives of those taking part.

Which branch of Imperial HQ? I had a brainwave. The Tokushu Joho Bu (TJB in our jargon) was our opposite number. Occasionally we would pick up a signal saying that they had intercepted a message from the Chinese, whose signal security was far from inscrutable. Could it plausibly get Singapore to relay a message on to Rangoon? It was worth looking into.

I was suddenly aware of two conflicting emotions. First came the excitement of using my wits and getting my teeth into something worthwhile and out of the ordinary. Even this discussion with a Colonel on equal terms was rare enough to be flattering.

But a mocking voice kept saying, "Don't be a fool. If you get mixed up with this daft scheme you may as well order your coffin now. Swallow your pride. Back out while there's still time."

Certainly the unofficial Army motto was 'Keep out of trouble. Never volunteer for anything.' But there was no time for agonising; I had an eight-hour shift ahead of me.

Our unit was a big affair with a staff of over a thousand. The security area was housed in former university buildings some miles outside Delhi, on top of Anand Parbat, 'The Hill of Happiness'. The lecture rooms, where most of us worked in teams of ten or so, were square and high. Many had a huge old-fashioned fan in the ceiling, which revolved just fast enough to give gentle breeze without swishing our papers on to the floor or disturbing the fat pigeon who sat on the blade and spent his life placidly going round and round. When the fan stopped he stayed there just the same, giddy or not.

In hot weather the temperature rose to 120° in the shade, but there in central India the humidity was generally so low that it felt like a pleasantly warm day in England. When it did become humid the windows were opened fully and woven screens were inserted in their place, which the local women cooled by constantly ladling water on to them. The gentle plash of water and the low murmur of their voices blended with the heat to give an overpoweringly soporific effect.

When the monsoon was close the humidity rocketed up and 'prickly heat' made people foul-tempered. The storm clouds would draw nearer each day, and eventually would arrive and break in sheets of water and fierce silver lightning in the thundery purple sky. Then, if you were off duty, you took off everything and rushed outside to dance in the torrential rain, celebrating the sense of release.

I made my way up the dusty path, now becoming crowded as the shifts changed. People of every service, rank and colour were coming and going in ones and twos, and I exchanged greetings with Noakes, who was coming off duty; we both worked on 2244. "Usual stuff," he grunted. I reached the top of the stony hill, showed my pass and entered the security area for the 1600–2400 shift.

Someone said, "Have you seen the notice? The CO's getting cold feet." Several others were studying it.

'*In view of the recent disappearance and presumed death of two WEC officers*' – there was no need to tell us who they were – '*all personnel are reminded that they are not to use the road through Karel Bagh as a short cut in journeys between here and Delhi. Officers visiting New Delhi on or off duty are not at present required to carry sidearms, but those on other journeys are to wear them at all times.*'

"He must love us after all," said one sardonic voice. I was not anxious to be reminded of the Karel Bagh incident, having used the route regularly before this. In practice it was difficult to persuade a tonga-driver not to take the short cut, and if he did it was equally difficult to jump out of a fast-moving tonga without injury. There was no doubt that it was an unsavoury place for British servicemen, especially with anti-British feeling on the increase.

The previous shift had left several partly-broken signals on my desk, with texts which had been mangled in enciphering, or transmitting, or somewhere along the line. I was soon immersed in the job. The restored texts read:

'Lieutenant Hitomura is leaving Singapore for Manila today.' Send that to the card-index people to see if we knew him at either place. What was he up to?

'12 Air Ferrying Unit is to move from Saigon to Moulmein at once.' Was it indeed? That would be to compensate for their recent losses of aircraft in Burma, so we must watch their moves closely.

One: Find 12 AFU where it appeared in the card index, and trace its recent history;

Two: Suggest photo-reconnaissance of Moulmein airfield, and a possible attack;

Three: Tell the RAF as soon as we knew more.

I took this one straight through to the Jap Air Route Unit room next door. Sutton presided over 'Peter's Popsies', a bevy of cheerful Indian girls who plotted the movements of these aircraft reinforcements. Glittering rows of teeth in seven dark faces – they were mostly from southern India – broke into smiles as if they had never seen a man before. Sutton was on the phone, so I gave it to the team leader, Sergeant Khosla – 'my chief mechanic' as he called her. "Very good, sir. It will be a pleasure." Her eyes flashed 'Hello' at me. I retreated to my pile of messages.

'Last message 358207 indecipherable; please repeat.' This proved to be one that we had read without difficulty, so thumbs down for some unknown Japanese cipher clerk.

'Serviceability report from 64 Hikosentai (Air Regiment): fifteen aircraft fully operational, one undergoing maintenance, one unserviceable with undercarriage damaged on landing, two destroyed by enemy fighter attack.' An Air Regiment originally consisted of forty or more aircraft, so if they were down to less than twenty they were in a bad way. The call-sign showed that the signal was from Magwe to Rangoon, so that told us, if we didn't know already, that 64 Air Regiment was now at Magwe. More work for the RAF.

'Please authorise immediate dispatch of spare engines ...'

I was glad to be interrupted. The Commanding Officer, Colonel Hartley-Kerr, wanted me in his office. Preston was with him, so any qualms that this sudden summons might have produced were short-lived.

"You are going on special detachment," said H-K without enthusiasm. He must have been overruled from on high. He never liked losing staff or even lending them, though he showed little enough interest in us when we were around.

"Things are beginning to move," Preston explained. "Your CO is kindly lending you to us for a week or two. Pack what you need, including some warmer clothes, and bring your copy of the 2244 codebook with you, Japanese dictionary – anything in that line. You are authorised to have it with you as long as you wear it next to your skin and never go to sleep. I'll have my jeep at the mess in half an hour."

There are times when it is best to act first and ask questions later, especially if you are a Lieutenant and two Colonels are doing the thinking for you. I scuttled back to my room, settled my mess bill, packed my valise, paid my bearer, Abdul Hamid, two weeks wages in advance, and was ready just in time.

"Good man. This is my driver and assistant, Sergeant Lewis; he has full security clearance. Put your kit in the front and we can talk shop in the back. We are spending a few days at Ranchi. I've got three seats on a Dakota and you can sleep in the plane if you are stoical enough. Meanwhile, this is what is happening.

"The Supremo and the General are giving this half-baked idea of yours top priority. We are going to put it in the oven and see how it turns out. It's the only one we've got and time is running out. We're getting a small team together to look at every aspect of it, pick holes in it, improve it and make it work. Every day counts."

We were running through New Dehli, past that gargantuan Lutyens creation, the Secretariat. Its sheer bulk was impressive, but by dwarfing everyone and everything in sight it became absurdly grandiose. The contrast of its vast, calculated landscape with the teeming alleys of Old Delhi was too extreme. Instead of elevating the spirit, as he had presumably intended, it squashed it flat.

Past the racecourse and out to the airfield. Lewis knew the short cuts, so there was only a brief check at the gate before we drove across to a plane on the perimeter track. We climbed up, put our kit on the floor and settled on the slippery seats that ran the whole length of the fuselage. I then realised that when Preston said 'three seats on a Dakota', he meant he had laid on a Dakota for only three people. Clearly the Supremo's top priority could move mountains.

"GHQ can pick up their jeep for themselves, Lewis. Hold on to this infernal seat until we're airborne."

Those troop-carrying Dakotas really were primitive. Until the tail-wheel came off the ground – few tricycle undercarriages in those days, remember – the whole affair bumped along with us gripping the seats so as not to land in a heap in the tail. Fortunately we were a light load compared with the dozens that were often squashed in, so before long we were at flying-level, with the lights of Delhi disappearing below us.

"Missed your dinner, didn't you? So did we. Lewis, the banquet."

Lewis was a short, versatile and imperturbable Welshman. He and Preston were obviously old friends, and there was no nonsense about pretending that he had a one-man Sergeants' mess further down the plane. He served our corned-beef sandwiches as if they were caviar, and filled our beakers from a coffee thermos with the elegance of a sommelier. One taste, however, and it proved to be chicken soup.

"Ah," said Preston, "a rare nose, a fine poultry bouquet, a formidable after-taste. I fancy that this comes from the southern slopes of the farmyard. Lewis, you have excelled yourself."

We washed that down with tinned fruit cocktail and real coffee. Preston produced a hip flask and we shared some fiery brandy. Lewis went forward to check our times with the pilots.

"Marvellous man, Lewis. Got me out of a fix in Libya. Hidden depths to him. Writes sonnets, very good ones. Now, the scheme is this. The General and I are bringing this team together at Ranchi where nobody can interrupt us. We'll have someone there from signals, someone from the RAF and others to follow. You will represent the crypto side."

"I've a nasty feeling that I'm going to be outranked. Are you sure you wouldn't be better off with one of the big guns from our units?"

"Nonsense. You had the brainwave – if it is a brainwave, as I very much hope – and you are now the proud father. We can't go selling the baby to anyone else. Nobody is going to pull rank in this outfit. If anyone tries, let me know. If the idea is a starter I shall rapidly commandeer any extra people we need and we shall plan the mission in detail. The team selected will then carry it out. The first thing is to find any flaws before the Japs do. Understood? Now we'll try to get some sleep in this buzz-box."

But before we could move our kit the pilot called us forward. "Don't miss this, Colonel. The Taj Mahal by moonlight."

We squeezed into the cockpit. Agra lay straight ahead, the river glinted below, and there was Shah Jehan's marble tomb standing cool and clear in the moonlight, Kipling's 'ivory gate through which all good dreams pass'. I quoted it hesitantly at Preston. He came back with "Dreams out of the ivory gate, and visions before midnight.' You know that one? Sir Thomas Browne, 300 years before Kipling pinched his idea."

One of the long pools reflected a slender minaret until the shadow of our aircraft stole across it. A moment later it had disappeared beneath us, and we laid out our bedding rolls on the corrugated floor, did our best to ignore the raucous noise, and slept fitfully.

Day Two:
Agnew Intervenes

It seemed only a few minutes later that we were landing at Ranchi in Bihar province. It stands on a plateau surrounded by plains, jungle, rivers and lakes, all of which had served for some years as training areas for British, Indian and even Chinese troops. After the long flight it was good to stretch our legs and breathe fresh air.

The jeep took us through the straggly town, whose main street was lined with European-style shops. An Army convoy was causing an immense traffic jam, and we turned down a narrow side street to avoid it. It was choked. Tailors squatted on the pavement to work their antiquated sewing machines. Pedestrians, cyclists and gharri-drivers fought noisily but good-humouredly for a way through the jewellers, cotton and silk merchants, scribes, food-sellers and fortune-tellers who also struggled to do business. We were given a reasonably clear passage; anti-British feeling seemed not to have reached here yet.

Outside a Hindu temple was a dusty garden in which a pye-dog sat, languidly nibbling a wallflower. A derelict banana-yellow van without tyres bore the legend 'NORTH INDIA PARTS COMPANY' in vivid purple letters. "What do you suppose?" Preston wondered. "Continental drift or a separatist movement?"

We were staying some miles outside the town, where Preston had taken over a small rest-house with woods above it and fields and a stream below: a sort of transplanted Swiss idyll.

He must have moved fast the previous day, for we were not the first to arrive. The RAF had sent Taylor, a Flight-Lieutenant of about thirty; dark-haired but balding, with a florid complexion and decidedly plump. He sported a handlebar moustache, something still greatly in vogue with fighter pilots in Britain, but an incongruous affectation in Asia. He stubbed out a cigarette, heaved himself out of his chair, and gave us a proprietorial but inquisitive welcome. What was going on? Where were his aircrew? Who were all these comics in khaki? He had expected an all-RAF team.

Preston had shown me his dossier in the plane: in peacetime a successful insurance salesman. He had the gift of the gab all right. He was well spoken of as a pilot, and had once brought his plane back safely despite flying into one of the wires the Japanese stretched across valleys to discourage low-level attacks on their river shipping. Apparently he had a high turnover of navigators, and his physical condition was rated as only fair; his last medical examination had been a close shave.

The signals people had chosen a Captain Stubbs, gawky, diffident and immediately likeable. Tousled black hair and heavy-rimmed glasses gave him a studious look. He had been a BBC engineer before the war, and was now trying to improve radio networks in the appalling conditions of north Burma. As we talked he began awkwardly filling his pipe.

"I'm sure they sent the wrong m-man." Jerk. "There's another Stubbs in the signals who's always" – jerk – "getting m-mixed up with me. They even sent me his pay chit once." He fumbled in his pockets and eventually brought out matches. "He's in some special duties unit." The first match broke; the second spluttered and went out. "I bet they m-meant him," – the third flared up and he puffed vigorously – "not me." A cloud of smoke enveloped him. Taylor's masterful manner seemed to have made him uneasy too, even after Preston had taken him on one side to set the scene and reassure him that he was the right man.

We breakfasted together. Taylor had second helpings but Stubbs hardly touched his; I could see a Laurel and Hardy pattern emerging. Preston had an Army signalman attached to us, and after sending off a signal to Fourteenth Army HQ he called us together.

"I'm expecting a Jap linguist soon – a Jap speaker, I should have said. Martyn here is the Jap crypto man, Stubbs is the signals wallah, and Taylor represents the RAF. We won't wait."

Taylor interrupted. "Excuse me, Colonel. They told me that I was being sent to lead an RAF team."

"Then I'm afraid your briefing was hopelessly wrong. You are the only RAF member so far, and I am in charge of the team until further notice. Now let's get on."

He gave a brisk thumbnail sketch of my plan, as he now called it.

"Another thing to remember is that while we're here everything is Top Secret. Officially we're here on leave. There are two divisions in training around us, and a lot of odds and sods as well, so we don't need a security area, booby traps and so forth, at least for now. The Bihari servants seem incorruptible but we'll still run no risks with them. Is that quite clear? Lieutenant-Colonel Agnew is coming over after lunch to offer ALFSEA's help in making our plans."

There was no hint of sarcasm, yet it was at once clear that he regarded this as an unwelcome intrusion. Allied Land Forces, South-East Asia, was a headquarters at Calcutta between Mountbatten, the Supremo in Ceylon, and Slim, the commander of the Fourteenth Army in Burma. Their function was to supervise and support Slim without interfering in details, but empire-building was as popular a sport with generals as with politicians. We had all heard rumours of friction. So Agnew's visit would be at best a mixed blessing, and at worst a hell of a nuisance.

"He will not be staying here but prefers to commute from Ranchi. Meanwhile we have plenty to think about. Now, what are your reactions to the plan? Stubbs, what about the signals side? If we put a trained operator into Malaya, can he impersonate a Jap operator in Singapore sending a signal to Rangoon?"

Stubbs' pipe had gone out again. He hesitated.

"Come on. Let your hair down. I shan't eat you if you're wrong."

"There are a lot of snags, sir," he began cautiously. Lewis started taking notes. "Your operator will have to learn all the Japanese frequencies, call signs, procedures, schedules and such-like, and use them absolutely convincingly. There's the crypto side, too, that I can't answer for. The biggest stumbling block is this: he'll have to m-mimic what we call the fist or handwriting of the Singapore operator – that means his personal rhythm and touch on the Morse key – so accurately that the regular Rangoon operator who receives it won't immediately know it's different and smell a rat." He shifted uneasily as if the problems were his fault. "And if the *real* Singapore operator is listening too, which is normal practice, I hate to think what he'll do when he realises that someone is trying to mimic his fist."

"You mean he'll get instant schizophrenia? That's a fine way to win the war. What can we do?"

"There may be a way round. Remember my experience is with large static units with fixed aerials and operators on regular schedules. That's what the Rangoon set-up will be like. But the clandestine agents are one-man-band characters with portable sets and completely different procedures. The M-Malayan stuff is all Greek to me."

"A felicitous phrase. Taylor, how would you fancy flying an aircraft to Rangoon and back, including a short stop at the airfield there?"

Taylor drew heavily on his cigarette and stared at him.

"What aircraft, Colonel? Are we disguising one of ours or stealing one of theirs? Can we refuel at the far end? How many people are we carrying? We'd need a fair-sized machine, at a guess."

"Probably five or six. If we find a Japanese plane for you, in decent running order, how long will you need to learn to fly it? You won't have long."

"The only big Jap planes I've seen at close quarters are Mitsubishi bombers. They are bigger than my Beaufighter but lighter; they leave out the armour-plate and the frills. The actual flying should be straightforward once I've got the hang of it, but I can't read Jap instruments and controls. I'll need my personal translator."

Preston grunted. "Very funny. Now try this one. If we flew from Calcutta to Rangoon, pretending to have come from Singapore, what would be the best route each way to avoid trouble?"

Taylor didn't hesitate. He strode over to the big map[*] and sketched out a short straight line and then a great sweeping curve, giving a confident running commentary.

"We fly down the coast to Cox's Bazaar, gentlemen, and there we fill our tanks up to the brim. Then we head out to sea, because there's a row of enemy airfields spaced out all the way down the coast: here, and here, and here. We curve round and come in north of the Andamans, sneaking through this gap, and gradually turn north to give the impression that we've come from Singapore. That must be nigh on a thousand miles. We take another route back, depending on the local weather, in case they rumble us after we've left Rangoon."

The man might be smug but he was a good tactician. And he had said 'us' all the time; Stubbs had left himself out.

"Good. let's leave the finer details for now. Martyn next: how do we send our naughty signal?"

"There are two sides to it. Stubbs and I can plan the signals and crypto stuff for Rangoon. But Colombo is the place to tell us about the clandestine radio business. They left people behind when Singapore fell and they've dropped more in since. It's quite on the cards that they've got someone in Malaya who could help, or else someone standing by for the next drop. He'd know all about the small radios and the territory."

"You mean the Force 136 mob? Of course. You suggested that yesterday and it slipped my mind." He ruminated, stroking his chin. "There's one snag. We don't usually tell agents more than they need to know, in case they're captured. In this case it might be worth the risk. He'll put his heart into it more if he has some notion what we are up to."

He bustled out to find the signalman. I caught sight of Lewis's notebook. Besides listing the things to do he had drawn a shrewd

---

* (See map of Burma, page 154)

17

caricature of Preston: the slightly hooked nose, the glint of his eyes, and one slightly raised eyebrow. He was now sketching Stubbs. The tufty hair and strong spectacles transformed him into an owl, and now the owl was puffing at a pipe. Preston came back, looking pleased.

"I've been cutting corners. Item one, the General agrees to our taking the risk of briefing the operator. He will clear that with the Supremo. Item Two, Colombo will be flying the operator up here pretty damn quick."

Taylor lit a new cigarette from the stump of the old and asked the question that had been taking shape in all our minds. "Colonel Preston, may we ask who's going on this trip?"

Preston surveyed a fly that was making its way across the ceiling. "It's a fair question but I can't answer it yet. I've several ideas but I'm keeping them under my hat for now. But get one thing absolutely straight, all of you. This operation has no more than a fifty-fifty chance of success. I don't mean the prospects of picking up the codebook; I mean the chance of surviving." The genial affability had gone from his voice for the first time. "Whoever flies in that plane will have to be in Japanese uniform and in disguise, otherwise the plan is a non-starter. So if it's ambushed, the normal prisoner-of-war rules do not apply. *That means the chop.* No use mincing words. Everyone will be a volunteer. Is that clearly understood?"

We understood all too well.

"Mind you," he went on more casually, "the Japanese attitude to the Geneva Convention is such that it might mean the chop even if we went in wearing British uniform, waving the Union Jack, with the Guards' band playing the National Anthem. I will now be monumentally indiscreet and say that I trust there will be no Guards officers on this picnic. They have brought the art of dying bravely to perfection, but on this occasion it will be more helpful, as well as more pleasant, to stay alive. So no heroics."

Perhaps I should explain this part of the Bushido tradition. Death in action was considered glorious; capture was the ultimate degradation. So a Japanese warrior in a hopeless situation had to commit suicide with the sword. It was no accident that their officers still carried swords into battle. And when they took prisoners, whom they regarded as beneath contempt, they often beheaded them – or worse. Yes, we would pause before volunteering.

The tradition contained one other bizarre feature. Before suicide, whether probable or certain – for example before the aircraft attacks that they called *kamikaze* or 'divine wind' – it was customary to compose a short mystical poem. One of the most celebrated was by Admiral Onishi, who invented the *kamikaze* tactic. In elegant calligraphy it read:

In blossom today, then scattered,
Life is so like a delicate flower;
How can one expect the fragrance
To last for ever?

None of us looked likely to write a poem before a mission, whether we rated our chances high or low. On the contrary, Lewis was doodling. A burly Taylor sat in his cockpit, waving a flag. As I watched, he acquired first a halo, then a Japanese squashy hat and drooping moustache, and a rising sun began to adorn the flag.

Preston went on, "But I've dodged Taylor's question. I have to pick a team of volunteers for the General to approve, and do it fast. We haven't yet decided how big a team we need. Any suggestions?"

Taylor again took the initiative: we needed a pilot and co-pilot and they could see to the navigation. Also a radio-operator, who might as well be an air-gunner too. If he could navigate or be a reserve pilot, so much the better.

I reminded him that we must have a fluent speaker of perfect idiomatic Japanese, capable of looking, sounding and behaving exactly like an enemy officer, to take delivery of the codebook itself. He would do the actual talking, probably in the guise of a Japanese general, and this was really the most demanding role to fill. "And it's no use looking at me," I protested; "my Japanese is written, and that's practically a separate language from what they speak."

"The Jap-speaking mock general is on order," said Preston "but I think we need someone else to make sure that what they give us really is the new 2244 book, not a lump of wood wrapped up prettily. That makes five: pilot, co-pilot, Jap-speaker, crypto man and a jack-of-all-trades."

"I should like to be pilot," Taylor said. "It's a neat scheme but it needs a confident chap who knows his way about Burma to fly this crate."

"If you really need a separate person to check the book, I'd like to volunteer," I added. "I know a lot of the old book by heart."

"Good for you both. I can't say yes or no at this stage but I'll keep the offers open. I can let Stubbs off the hook. Like Lewis and me, he hasn't got the right qualifications."

"I only wish I had," said Stubbs resignedly.

The head bearer, Adur, served lunch. He had deep-set, half-hooded eyes, which combined with a toothy grin to suggest a friendly lizard. Preston chatted to him in the local dialect. "They're an aboriginal race, and as tough as old boots. I've known Adur on and off for years. He cleans our rooms, and if you lock them – which you should do – he, but nobody else, has a key. His wife does the laundry and will destroy your shirts less rapidly than most dhobis. His so-called cousin is the cook, and a good one."

"Who is the round-faced one who's just gone out?"

"That's his Number Two, a recent arrival called Hira Lal. Adur says he's a Christian. I'm no infidel, but Indians and Christianity don't always mix. In Calcutta I've known some saintly ones, but in the south they are so conscious of impending forgiveness that they think they can get away with anything. When they say 'turn the other cheek', they mean 'turn a blind eye while I pinch your camera and flog it in the market'. Still, this one had some good chitties, and his predecessor had gone a bit gaga, so he'll probably do. I only wish he didn't wear that constant simpering smile. I suggest you lot go for a walk after lunch. We'll meet at 1600 for tea and get down to business again. Lieutenant-Colonel Agnew and I should have finished our deliberations by then. Be on your best behaviour and don't underrate the significance of his visit. There are some big noises at ALFSEA."

Taylor looked at the local map. "My station MO says I've got to take more exercise. Anyone care to come for a walk? There looks to be a track up through the woods."

Stubbs was going down to the nearby village to buy some necessities that he'd forgotten to bring, so we left him to it and made our way up the hillside. The combination of hot sun and hot curry made us grateful for the trees.

The path joined a track and the slope lessened. An oxcart laden with baulks of timber creaked down towards us and the driver gave us open greetings, very different from the reactions of townspeople. Before long we came out at the top of the woods and saw a great sweep of heathland like a Scottish moor, with a group of tall firs at the top.

"What else is on our agenda?" asked Taylor, who seemed more relaxed now that he knew the set-up.

"There's drafting a signal that will do the trick at Rangoon, getting into their network without blowing the gaff, disguise, Jap uniforms, not to mention finding a plane, which seems a tall order. Can you see yourself flying one of their bombers into Rangoon? And getting out again?"

"God knows, but it's in the best Hollywood tradition. Errol Flynn at the controls, Clark Gable as co-pilot, Spencer Tracy in the turret, Peter Lorre as the Japanese officer. All very colourful."

I added, "And a grand triumphal march to welcome us back. But don't forget they'd invent some phoney love interest and the usual personality clash between the pilots, preferably over the target. They both want the same woman."

He grunted, and we plodded towards the trees.

21

"Everything hangs on getting the right man for the bogus Jap general," I suggested. "There can't be many candidates, and most of them are in Burma as intelligence officers. But it's one thing to speak Japanese well enough to interrogate prisoners, and another to pass yourself off as a Jap officer."

"Frankly I'm not much worried about the intelligence jokers. This democratic set-up is all very well for laying the foundations and Preston is a harmless old buffer, but we need a really good RAF staff officer to coordinate the whole flying operation, or this will be another Army Shambles, First Class."

An extraordinary sight was just ahead: there was a hoopoe standing in the short grass, and while we watched it raised its absurd plume and posed for us. I am no ornithologist but I knew it at once. At school we had translated Aristophanes' comedy *The Birds*, and the hoopoe had formed the frontispiece – a dull engraving compared with the gaudy creature that was still posing. Then it ran, not hopped, along the ground, said "Hoo-poo-poo" to us twice, rose into the air on black-and-white striped wings, and flew off.

"That's a bird of ill omen," Taylor pronounced.

I felt just the opposite. This Arabian Nights character, who had been a forgotten grey stereotype until a minute before, had turned into dazzling reality. What could be more auspicious?

We reached the top and squatted in the shade of the trees. We could see for miles, and there was no sign of human activity except for a smoky blur away to the east, which must be Calcutta. There was a soft breeze and a glaring blue sky with a few very white clouds.

Up here it was hard to remember Preston and the others. As for the Rangoon scheme, it was ridiculous. No group of sane people could stitch together such a jumble of fanciful notions and call it a plan. Yet absurd as it was, it still haunted my imagination and, I thought from his sudden silence, Taylor's. Or was it just a film in glorious Technicolour?

I heard the hoopoe again. Down at Colombo Mountbatten had chosen a hardly less extravagant bird, the phoenix, as his crusading symbol for South-East Asia Command. What had these two improbable creatures to do with the book or the film ...?

Taylor woke me up. "Dozing off when on duty? I take a dim view of that. It's time to get back."

We ambled down the hill in the shade; where the trees ended we turned towards the rest-house, half a mile away across the curving top of a field. It was being tilled by a group of really voluptuous Bihari women, dusky-skinned and full-bosomed, wearing only long brilliantly coloured skirts. They waved cheerfully as we walked past, and we waved back, resolutely keeping the officer sahib's regulation stiff upper lip, though Taylor made some luridly appreciative comments. Further on we came across their husbands, squatting round a hubble-bubble while their wives and daughters did the work.

We came back across the rough lawn. Preston was reclining in an enormous bamboo armchair, a parody of all Colonel Blimps. Even the chair was a parody, needing a man each side to carry it with its extending footrest, adjustable canopy, thick green cushions and trays for drinks.

"Well, you lazy blighters. Here we are, carrying the cares of the Empire while you go cavorting round the countryside, ogling the dark-eyed houris."

Agnew came out, as brimful with conversation as a society hostess. He had lived in Rangoon for six years before the Japanese arrived, and he clearly expected everything to return to normal when the war ended: the British club, the servants, the golf course, the landed-gentry attitudes. We remembered Preston's injunction to behave ourselves, and were suitably docile.

Where did we come from? Where had we been at school? Did we know General Thing, who farmed thereabouts? What did we do in civilian life? Did we ride? Did we shoot? "Only Japanese," I said gently, "and not for pleasure." The teapot, another great Edwardian relic, was borne out ceremoniously, Adur retired and Stubbs came up the track, mopping his brow.

Preston started the discussion. "Things are moving. The chap from Colombo, an army captain called Wallace, will be here first thing tomorrow. Stubbs, I want you to stay here until tomorrow evening at least, and then I'll have to send you back to your unit.

"Now, our tame general will be a Captain Henderson, an intelligence officer with 2 Division, very busy with interrogation. He's said to be a top-notch Japanese linguist and a keen amateur actor, which could be useful. He should be here today. I hope to goodness that he's going to fit happily into our team, because this isn't a walking-on role. He has the central part in our charade, without offence to you others."

Agnew raised his eyebrows slightly but said nothing. I knew Henderson, and said so. From time to time people from our unit went down to old Delhi when they had any Japanese prisoners who had been signal or cipher clerks. They were flown back there for detailed interrogation, and held at the Red Fort. I had done joint interrogations with Henderson sometimes. He knew the spoken language well but not our technical terms; I was the other way round.

It may be surprising, but these prisoners fell over themselves to tell us about their secrets. The other side of the Bushido tradition meant that when any Japanese were captured – and for a long time very few were – they were amazed at being left alive, let alone decently treated. Those who were specialists were gratified to find people who spoke their language and shared their speciality, and since they were still convinced that their codes were unbreakable, they treated us almost as colleagues. We would move on to an innocent question: "Let me see, was that when we began to encipher the indicator?" – notice the artful 'we', not 'you' – and they were only too happy to bring us up to date.

I had a clear memory of Henderson's role in these interrogations and the discussions that followed. He would hold back as if uninterested, and then intervene dramatically with a telling word or two. He would be a powerful addition to the team, but not always a comfortable partner.

"I must tell you that there is an unfortunate lack of unanimity about certain aspects of our plan," Preston was saying. "Our friends at Calcutta" – permitting himself a mere hint of disapproval – "have various suggestions for improving it. Will you please describe them, Agnew?"

Agnew straightened his trousers, placed his fingertips together and gave us his mirthless smile.

"General Greatorex is not happy, gentlemen, about three things. First, the question of the aircraft. We think it unlikely that an enemy aircraft can be acquired and we doubt both the ethics and the expediency of using it. Strictly speaking, the use of disguise, whether of personnel or of equipment, would mean that those taking part would be regarded as spies, not soldiers, and would be liable to immediate execution."

It was like a lecture to first-year law students.

"We've known that from the start," Taylor said. "We understand that anybody volunteering faces those risks."

Agnew pursed his lips. Interruptions were not to be encouraged.

"I am aware of that. My general considers that junior officers should not be exposed to the danger of volunteering for a mission which carries an unacceptably high risk. The second objection is that the use of a bogus signal would entail the risk of compromising the security essential to the activities of WEC at Delhi."

Preston glanced at me and I took the cue.

"We know that they are about to change the book anyway. That's the whole reason for us stealing the new one. So there's nothing to lose and everything to gain, especially at this stage of the campaign."

Agnew frowned. This came close to insubordination.

"You must accept the mature views of better-informed authorities, Martyn."

He blew his nose and tucked the handkerchief inside his cuff, Guards-fashion.

"Finally, the question of command has yet to be settled. At present no officer of sufficient seniority has been allocated to direct the operation. Until that matter has been resolved, General Greatorex cannot give his formal approval."

Stubbs had been looking more and more bewildered. "Excuse me, Colonel Agnew," he said mildly; "I'm lost. Does ALFSEA believe that everything in the scheme is wrong? They say it's improper to use a captured aircraft, but what's the point as they say we shan't find one anyway? They don't want junior officers volunteering, so how s..s..senior do officers have to be before they can, especially if there's nobody senior enough to command them? But anyway they don't want *anyone* to try to get a codebook that will help us to win in Burma, so where does the seniority issue come in? I thought it was unpatriotic to spread alarm and despondency? Or does that depend on seniority too?"

This gentle rebuke seemed to floor Agnew. Preston broke the long silence that followed. "Well, it's out of our hands. Our lords and masters will no doubt pronounce on these matters. Meanwhile there's a great deal to do and time is slipping away fast. I suppose the crypto people have no clue when the new book could come in?"

"Excuse me," said Agnew, standing and flicking imaginary dust from his jacket. "I'll leave you to deal with these technicalities."

A perfectly proper sentiment in itself, but from a Lieutenant-Colonel to a full Colonel it carried the condescending implication that he had better things to do, and was graciously leaving triviali-ties to a subordinate. As his jeep went down the drive I realised that I hadn't answered Preston.

"We've little to go on. The other material in the system is changed fairly often, but we had expected the book to last at least another year. Now they could give as little as a day's notice if they chose."

Preston scratched his head. "I see. What's this other material you mentioned? I thought there was just a codebook?"

"You're underestimating them, sir. This 2244 system has the codebook protected by two extra layers. It's all Top Secret, but everything else on this operation seems to be as well, so I'll happily explain if you authorise me to."

"I don't see why not. It concerns us all. Make it brief."

I explained it as succinctly as I could.

"Ye Gods, that's a formidable affair. You say you lads can break this stuff?"

"Given enough signals traffic, people and time we certainly can. At present we're reading it as fast as the Japs, except when they change material."

Taylor, whose eyes glazed over whenever anything to do with intelligence was mentioned, broke in impetuously. "We're forgetting one vital thing. What fools we are."

Preston scowled. "Speak for yourself, Taylor. Do you mean you've just remembered something?"

"There's one thing we must have, sir, and that's up-to-date details of Mingaladon airfield at Rangoon, if that's where we are doing this weird job. Suppose they've installed more of those diabolical wires I had an argument with at Toungoo. We need to know that before we arrive on their doorstep. A high-altitude photo-reconnaissance Mosquito is the answer. It can get up to nearly 40,000 feet and it's fast enough to leave a Zero behind. I suggest a daily flight, taking in one or two other airfields as well so as not to give the game away."

"An obvious precaution, Taylor. It is already laid on."

A jeep turned off the road and came up our track. Lewis was at the wheel and beside him I recognised Henderson, tall and fair-haired, with prominent cheekbones. His ice-blue eyes held a steady impenetrable gaze that gave nothing away; his Scots brogue emerged only when he became worked-up – which was rare. People who didn't know him thought that the cool stare and the few words meant arrogance. They were wrong. He was more severe with himself than with others – but the moment any important issue came up he could rasp some very pithy comments.

He greeted me with a paralysing handshake. Preston gave him a warm welcome. "What's this, a crown? You're down on my list as captain, not major."

"It came through a few days ago, quite out of the blue."

"This calls for a celebration when we've something stronger than tea to drink it in. Sit down and join the team. Adur," in a great bellow, "we need more tea. I'll brief you on the progress we've made so far and Lewis can check that I leave nothing out."

He ran through the plot in rapid detail. Henderson was obviously intrigued but said not a word.

"So you see there's a hell of a lot to do. We're still without an aircraft. That matter is in hand but time is running out. Once we get it we mark it conspicuously to show how important it is. Even Greatorex can hardly expect us to fly into Mingaladon with RAF markings. Might as well commit suicide here. That plane will have been flown by both pilots and you will all have had at least one trial flight in it. You will also have had intensive personal preparation: firearms, disguise, uniforms, language practice, and you will be in first-class physical condition. Taylor, I tell you frankly that you have some way to go. You're overweight and puffing like a grampus. See to it. What else? I want you all to memorise Japanese insignia of rank from that chart and test each other until you've got them perfect. I shall teach you how to give Jap salutes. Nobody will have a shred of non-Japanese private property on that plane. You will all *be* Japanese, not just pretend to be. The flight itself will take place along this route so as to arrive at Rangoon smack on time, in the best Yamamoto tradition."

He stopped. There was a shocked silence. He and we had realised at the same instant that this was an inauspicious comparison. Admiral Yamamoto, who had masterminded the slaughter at Pearl Harbor, had later been shot down by the Americans after they had broken the JN 25 signal giving the timetable for his tour of inspection. His well-known insistence on punctuality had helped them to plan his interception.

"Gentlemen, kindly accept my apologies for that deplorable gaffe. I was of course referring solely to Yamamoto's obsession with split-second timing. And his plans became known. Yours will remain secret, and your punctuality will be logical, not obsessive. I trust I may be forgiven?

"To resume, we shall arrange things so that our plane will be on the ground at Rangoon for the shortest possible time. As soon as you've got the book you will return by the safest route. You will also go prepared to kidnap the Jap officer if he has the book but is reluctant to hand it over."

"Is it fair to ask how we stand over General Greatorex and Colonel Agnew," ventured Taylor, "or is that stepping into a minefield?"

Preston mused, puffing his cheeks out, then relaxed. "This affair stands or falls on being frank. I'm extremely vexed that ALFSEA have seen fit to come bumbling into our plans. It's an ominous sign, as Stubbs observed, that their objections have no logical connection with each other, which suggests that someone is being awkward for the sheer hell of it. ALFSEA comes between Mountbatten and Slim in the command structure, as you may know, so Mountbatten can trump their aces while he's around, but when he's not they can trump Slim's. Mountbatten's in Washington – I didn't tell you that – so they have a free hand for a few days. My feeling is that he will back us on the signals security argument and the choice of a plane because, as Martyn pointed out, there's no rival plan and the prize justifies the risks."

"So we don't need to worry about ALFSEA?" Henderson sounded doubtful.

"If I know Greatorex he will have another card up his sleeve, which he will play while the Supremo is still away. We haven't seen the end of this skirmishing, gentlemen. Hold your hats on and don't worry. Now let us adjourn. We need to stop talking shop for a while, or we shall become hag-ridden." He glanced at his watch. "Let us meet about 1830 to give us time for some idle chatter before dinner. I cannot guarantee that there will be no business to discuss, but we will at least keep it in its place."

The rest-house was the standard wooden bungalow that the Public Works Department built in tens of thousands all over India, in different lengths. Single rooms opened on to a long verandah, along which the tree-rats, a local variety of squirrel, cavorted. Behind each room was a tiny cubicle containing a canvas bath and thunderbox. The one larger room did triple duty for eating, relaxing and planning. Out at the back was a separate block for kitchen and servants' quarters.

I went to my room, bathed, changed and sat outside in the early evening light. A peahen was strutting across the rough lawn, giving an occasional raucous contralto screech. From the village below there rose sweetly scented wood smoke as they cooked their evening meals, and an intermittent drumming suggested that some local ceremony or celebration was going on.

I thought about the signal yet again – I couldn't get it out of my head. To carry maximum weight it *must* purport to come originally from imperial HQ in Tokyo and specifically from our counterpart the TJB. That was settled. But what plausible reason could there be for having the signal to Rangoon relayed via Singapore, not sent direct from Tokyo? If our flight could be passed off as part of a round trip, picking up codebooks here and there, and calling at Singapore before Rangoon, with the unspoken implication that we might be going on to Bangkok or Saigon, everything would be quite believable. But how to prevent Rangoon from checking the authenticity of this highly unusual signal with their colleagues at Singapore?

Of course: by *ordering* them not to, 'for security reasons'. Those same orders could also enforce absolute secrecy and isolation on the airfield. We could specifically command the hypothetical Major running the signals unit to come to the aircraft alone. We could order him not to breathe a word to a soul. We could even instruct him to destroy our signal when it was finished with.

The sheer audacity of the idea intoxicated me, although it seemed to have invented itself. The more secret, unusual and imperious the message, the more convincing it would be. It would start with one of those patriotic exhortations the Japanese had been issuing so plentifully since the tide had turned against them, and finish with a hint of a personal involvement in the glorious victory that was just round the corner. Ever since the failure of their Imphal siege we had become increasingly familiar with that vocabulary. The uniqueness of our message might also help to explain away any oddity in our signals procedure. Feeling rather pleased with this I went to see what Stubbs thought about it.

He brought me down to earth with a bump. "Don't you see? The enemy operators all know each other's fists by heart. They'll be listening to the transmissions. The prelims will give the game away before they have a chance to reach your text. Either we can't mimic them well enough, or if we get it exactly right the man we are mimicking will know that it's a fake. So we are sunk either way. He'll rush off and report his suspicions to his superior officer before our ingenious explanations can be got across."

He seemed impatient that I still hadn't grasped the problem and its significance: either reaction would torpedo the whole scheme, betraying the bogus nature of the signal, alerting them to possible danger and destroying any chance of a second attempt. It would also sign the death warrant of the team and probably of our radio-operator.

I wandered outside again, bitterly disappointed, but still convinced that there was a way round. It was growing darker, and countless grasshoppers were whirring in the long grass. So, there was no hope that an outsider, even with the highest credentials, could fool the enemy signals people. That meant abandoning any pretence that our signal was coming from the normal Singapore HQ. We must accept that our operator was totally separate, and dream up a good reason for his existence. Everything about the message was going to be special, so we had to invent a Special Operator and unveil him plausibly to the enemy operators at both ends. And that had to be done not just at the start of the message but at the start of our transmission – with the great advantage that now we needn't worry about mimicking anyone's fist. All we had to do was to reproduce normal Japanese procedure. Walking on air, though still half prepared for another downfall, I joined the others.

Preston had made some headway too. He gave us a breezy summary.

"I have had a signal from Colombo promising to dispatch (their word) an American Naval Air Force lieutenant, one Thomas Coe, a pilot who is bilingual in Japanese and English. There is one obscure word in the text which you Jap-wallahs can interpret. He is a 'nisti' Jap. Does it mean nifty or nasty?"

Henderson and I were in a dead heat; I let him explain.

"Nisei, Colonel. There's one letter wrong. Nisei means that he's a second-generation American-born Japanese. The Yanks use a lot of them in intelligence work, especially interrogation."

"This chap was born in Honolulu, before the family moved to California. His father runs a chain of hardware stores, and after Pearl Harbor, Junior trained to become an engineer. He joined the Navy, became a fighter pilot and was in the Aleutians when the Japs attacked them. Apparently a Zero ran out of fuel and crash-landed on the beach, and he flew it back for examination, since when he has been evaluating captured aircraft all round the Pacific. His family name is Kohara, but so many Yanks mistook it for O'Hara that he abbreviated it to Coe. Like other nisei men – I see it spells it properly here – he is normally kept at least 200 miles from the front line, for his own security. I understand that applies to you too, at least in theory," looking at Henderson and me. Henderson nodded; nobody had told me.

"He has repeatedly volunteered to ignore that if necessary, and will do so again if invited to join our team. He is twenty-two, single, Catholic and plays baseball. The Americans are generous with their information as with all else. Any questions? Will he fit in? Is anyone here a Yankophobe?"

"Bloody Yanks or bloody Japs," muttered Taylor. "We could do worse." Henderson wryly suggested that if English, Scottish and Welsh could work together, anything was possible. This addition to our team would also solve Taylor's problem: how to read the controls and instruments of our long-awaited captured plane, and how to cope with any enemy radio messages during the flight.

Taylor grunted, "I hope to goodness he has flown something heavier than fighters since he left flying school." You could sense that he was preparing to regard Coe as a rival rather than a colleague.

Preston went on, "Coe is on his way via Colombo and should be here by tomorrow, not far behind Wallace, the chap we hope will send our signal.

"There's also some encouragement about the plane. The RAF can virtually guarantee us a Jap bomber which landed at Dohazari by mistake. But it needs some damage to be repaired and they are having to improvise spares, so it can't be ready yet. I've threatened them with the wrath of God if those repairs take a minute longer than necessary.

"We shall dine shortly and nobody will then talk shop. Afterwards, if you will allow me, I will introduce you to the delights and deceits of liar-dice."

Dinner was quite animated. We were now six: Preston, Henderson, Taylor, Stubbs, Lewis and me. Only Preston's unorthodox views and forceful personality could have contrived Sergeant Lewis's presence in what would otherwise have been an officers' mess. On a later occasion I heard him speak tartly to a major who challenged this. "Where do you draw the line? On a life raft? In the jungle? Do you believe in the caste system? On the parade ground it's a different matter; that's hierarchy or nothing. But let us admit a little humanity into our dealings with fellow human beings. And when I'm cashiered you can come and jeer." Taylor didn't look best pleased at having Lewis there, though as a fellow diner there was no doubt who fitted in better. God knows what Agnew would have made of it.

Preston was equally scathing about racial prejudice, 'the colour bar' as it was then called, and especially its adoption by the British in India. "What the devil difference does it make whether a man's skin is black, white, yellow or red? Do we have separate regiments for redheads or baldies? What we need to know is if they are good or bad, sane or daft, honest or deceitful. The only thing prejudice tells you is the character of the person who feels it.

"As for the typical British club here that admits British officers and their wives but excludes Indian officers and their wives on what it calls a matter of principle – if that's what they call a principle, God help them. When the Umpteenth Bhatpur Lancers, who couldn't field a polo team without a majority of Indian officers, win the match and then have to celebrate in two separate parties, bad luck to them."

Such outspoken views might have been less surprising in a disgruntled corporal or a socialist subaltern, or expressed much later. In a senior Army officer in the 1940s, above all in India, they were rare and refreshing – though there was a healthy tradition of eccentric colonels.

It seemed to occur above all after retirement: they took up Morris dancing, model railways and hand-loom weaving – notoriously un-warlike activities – so clearly they had had enough. Others believed in British Israelites and pyramidal inches. One became a Tibetan lama, and two others, clad in deep mourning, used to walk solemnly every year to Trafalgar Square to lay a wreath at the foot of the statue of Charles I on the anniversary of his execution.

"Indians are bloody wogs, just the same," Taylor muttered while Preston was deep in conversation.

Henderson and I talked about life before the war. He had studied modern languages at St Andrews and then become an Assistant Lecturer there in German. When the war caught up with him he joined the Engineers and went on a demolition course in which he learned how to blow up bridges, derelict railway lines and anything else that the County Council wanted removed free of charge. After Pearl Harbor, with few people who understood Japanese and therefore little prospect of carrying out intelligence work in the Far East, he went on one of the first courses in the spoken language at the School of Oriental and African Studies in London, affectionately known as the School of 'Orrible Studies. Eventually he came out to Burma to work with 2 Division.

"What did you do in your spare time, if any?"

"Acting. That's how I met my wife. We both had walking-on parts in the Merchant of Venice while we were students. She's now in the Wrens doing photographic interpretation. I'm trying to get her shifted to their branch out here, but it's like moving Stonehenge. What about you?"

"No wife, but I live in hope. I was still an undergraduate at Cambridge, studying Classics but spending far too much time on music. I got in two terms before being whisked off for the written Jap course at Bedford, and then went on to Bletchley Park before coming out here. You realise how bright the Services were for once? Modern linguists went into spoken Japanese; dead-language people did written. When you remember how many electrical engineers were retrained as cooks, and vice versa, it's a triumph of good sense over military tradition."

"I agree," said Preston, impetuously joining in. "I've always been out of step, and the Army doesn't care for it. It's a balancing trick. If I hadn't been unorthodox I'd still be a half-colonel. But if I hadn't been *so* unorthodox I might have been a general by now – right or wrong. Anyway we come into our own in wartime, whatever the Blimps think."

"What did you do before the war, sir?" Taylor asked when there was a lull in the conversation.

"Which war, boy? I was just old enough to catch the end of the 1914–18 affair in the Middle East. Bumped into Lawrence several times; a bright lad but as crooked as a corkscrew. When peace broke out I tried farming, but that was a flop because I didn't have enough capital. Then both my parents died in a car crash so I was on my own. I sold the house and started travelling across Europe on foot. I soon discovered that I was happiest off the beaten track, so after Athens I made for Istanbul and the Middle East. Kindly pass me that enticing basket of fruit, and have some yourselves.

"Let me see. I liked Iran, so I settled in Isfahan for a year to learn Farsi, looking at mosques and ruins, chatting to tribesmen, buying a lovely Tree of Life carpet dirt-cheap – probably stolen. Someone stole it back some weeks later. I even got across to Herat in Afghanistan. Then an invitation from a New Zealand cousin caught up with me, so I spent some time there helping him with sheep fanning, and doing some amateur mountain climbing on my free days.

"In 1937 it finally dawned on me that war was inevitable, so I came home cosily by Imperial Airways and joined a county regiment that would put up with my eccentricities, and soldiered my way along. Infantry ski instructing, a boring office job in Cairo, some cloak-and-dagger stuff with Jordanian tribesmen. Met the General when I was a major and he was a colonel. We got along well, so here I am. That's enough of that. How are you people getting on at the far end?"

"Finished some time ago, Colonel."

"Cheeky blighter," with that schoolboy grin. "Let's have coffee."

Afterwards, as threatened, he introduced us to liar-dice. Stubbs and I watched while the other four played. I've forgotten the details, but the principle, as in poker, was bluff. You hid a pair of dice in a leather cup and announced what their total was. Then you passed them on, hidden under the cup, to your neighbour, who had to do the same after looking at them – but always declaring a higher total. You often had to pretend to be telling the truth when you weren't and, more subtly, try to catch others out by pretending to be telling a lie when you weren't. If someone challenged you and you were telling the truth, you collected his chips. If you weren't, he collected yours.

What mattered was the face. Preston's registered hope or despair when he had no cause for either, thus luring the unwary to challenge him and bring about their downfall. Taylor's face was so mobile that it was hard to pin any one emotion on it. Henderson had a perfectly expressionless mask that gave nothing away, but he was not good enough at guessing the others' intentions. Lewis had the perfect poker face and he saw through the masks of the rest. They were not playing for cash, but his pile of chips grew steadily. It was Taylor he cleaned out first, then Henderson, then Preston.

Day Three:
Baiting The Trap

The next day I woke to hear aircraft engines. Hira Lal explained that Preston and Lewis had gone up the hill, and I ran along the edge of the field to see what was going on. They had lit a smoke flare to show the wind direction. The Dakota made a further run, a figure jumped out, his parachute opened, and he drifted down and made a clean landing. The plane circled again and dropped another parachute with a load under it.

Henderson caught me up as I went to meet them. Preston was greeting Wallace, the man from Force 136. "Very spectacular. I take it you're getting in some extra practice?"

"Yes, sir. It also saved time."

He was a tall, lean man, older than I had expected, with bright blue-green eyes in an elfin face crinkled by the sun and tanned yellow from intensive dosing against malaria. He seemed short of breath but not short of words.

"What's this other gear?"

"Mostly my radio set. We keep trying to find better ways of packing it so that it can fall down a ravine into a stream and still work. Today wasn't much of a test."

"Come down to the house and let these youngsters bring the stuff."

We breakfasted on the verandah, looking across the valley. Henderson had shaved carelessly, which was unusual; a red and white tuft of cotton wool clung to one cheek like a tiny cactus in the desert. The people in the fields had stopped working when they heard the plane so low. They would not have seen a parachute before, so there was plenty of excitement. Perhaps they were hoping for a repeat performance. Hira Lal seemed almost beside himself with curiosity, his teeth glistening in the full-moon face.

"Tell me about yourself, Wallace. Colombo didn't say much. How long have you been out East?"

"I came out to Malaya twelve years ago to learn forestry. I started as a dogsbody and gradually worked my way up till I was running a forest reserve in Pahang. Apart from the rain and the mosquitoes I loved it. It's a beautiful country if you are happy to be away from civilisation and can make convincing excuses for avoiding bridge parties on other people's estates. I spent my spare time watching butterflies. There are hundreds of different sorts, some as big as plates ..."

"Yes, exquisite. Let's move on. What came next?"

"After the Singapore fiasco I volunteered to stay on. Despite all the muddle I eventually caught up with a pack of Chinese gangsters further north in a part I didn't know. They had a camp right up in the hills beside a stream, and made a living by threatening to murder merchants who wouldn't pay up. Occasionally the Japanese would come looking for us but they never quite caught up, and we would go down and shoot up the military traffic and leave booby traps to tie down more troops. But the Chinese haven't any central organisation there. Everything happens in these local bands. None of them seem to know about any other group, and if they meet them they're as likely to shoot at them as at the Japanese, so it's a madhouse ..."

"When did you get out? How did you manage it?"

"By late '43 I'd got malaria and dysentery pretty badly. We got a message to Colombo on a radio that was on its last legs, like me. Eventually they carried me down to the west coast and I was picked up by a British submarine near Ipoh. All those coastal waters are so shallow that a sub can't get in close, so you have to paddle around in the gloaming, feeling horribly conspicuous, until you find each other.

"Anyway, that brought me back to Ceylon and after six weeks I was pretty fit. Then I learnt how to manage a radio properly and deal with my own ciphers, and went on other courses on firearms and explosives and whatnot, and now I'm raring to go back."

"Fine. Have they told you where they're dropping you?"

"Not exactly, but somewhere in Pahang again."

"Pahang my foot. We want you in Johore. Any objections?"

Wallace was taken aback. He thought before replying. "Frankly, sir, the place doesn't matter in itself, but all my contacts are in Pahang and we've set up local committees, agreed on sites for dropping zones, the lot. I want to get straight down to business. It's always tricky to start with, and they are touchy about newcomers. If you can find anyone else ..."

"No go, I'm afraid. I see your problem and I sympathise, but you'll have to lump it."

"Then I just hope there's a decent local organisation. I'm fed up with being governess and nurse and father-confessor as well as commander-in-chief of hundreds of cut-throats without any help."

"Quite right too. What the devil is it, Hira Lal?" He spoke more sharply than usual.

"You wanting more toast, sahibs?" He had been hovering near the table with his usual inane smile, and we waited while he cleared away some dishes and retreated to the kitchen.

"Now," said Preston "let me explain what we want you to do and why it's so important. As soon as you land ..." and he summarised our plans.

"Christ Almighty," Wallace exploded. "It's nothing to do with Force 136. You just want me to be your radio-operator for a funny signal?"

"Crudely put, yes. It's you or nobody. The scheme has got the Supremo's top priority, so I'm afraid you've got no option."

Wallace looked round at us, shrugged and gave in. "But can we get down to business straight away, please?"

"Certainly you shall. I want you and Stubbs to solve the Johore end of the signals problem by teatime at the latest. Henderson and Martyn will compose the final draft of the message so that you can take it back with you. Taylor, I haven't forgotten about you. As soon as Coe arrives you and he are to talk non-stop about flying; no reminiscences, just bright ideas for our flight. All of you will have to get a move on, but don't overlook any detail. Call me if you need a second opinion."

Preston had already given Henderson a summary of our plans and of the unwelcome message from Greatorex, but this was my first chance to explain to him in detail my idea for a signal that would accomplish all we wanted, simply by ordering Rangoon to provide it, and by emphasising patriotism, secrecy and absolute compliance in the most forceful terms. He saw the point at once.

"But joint texts are a nuisance. You're more used to that vocabulary than I am. You make the first draft using all their clichés. I'll pick holes in it with pleasure. Meanwhile I'll start practising my role as a Japanese general."

I was relieved that he thought the same about joint texts as I did, so I went to my room, got out my notes, my Kenkyusha dictionary and the codebook, and began. After an hour's work, this is what the English text looked like:

MOST SECRET

For the personal attention of the Commanding Officer, Signals Section, 5 Air Division Headquarters, RANGOON.

1. In the crucial operations now being carried out by Imperial forces the secrecy of our communications is of paramount importance. During a recent strategic withdrawal in the Great East Asia War some cryptographic material may have shamefully fallen into enemy hands. To obviate any risk of compromising signals security, Imperial HQ are taking stringent measures, including the bypassing of normal signals channels.

2. To guarantee absolute security the following instructions are to be scrupulously observed. The contents of this signal are to be known only to yourself and no communications on this subject are permitted inside or outside your own unit.

3. You are directed that the recently issued two-part codebook for system 2244 (04-shiki R 70718) is not repeat not to be brought into use. A replacement book will be distributed as soon as possible. Meanwhile you are to keep the current codebook (01-shiki M 21336) in use until further notice.

4. Your copy of R 70718 will be collected in person by Major-General Yamaji of Imperial HQ/Chuo Tokushu Joho Bu. He will arrive at Mingaladon airfield at 1315 hrs on (date). The following procedure will then be punctiliously observed:

a) You are to be ready at the airfield with the said book, having given a plausible explanation to the airfield authorities for any local arrangements.

b) No ceremonies whatever will take place. On arrival the aircraft will move to a secluded part of the airfield. Ground personnel must be kept clear. No refuelling will be required.

c) No air escort will be provided for his arrival or departure, but our aircraft in the area are to be warned, without detailed explanation, to recognise and avoid his aircraft. For the sake of security no route details are being given.

d) You alone are to drive to the aircraft. Major-General Yamaji will identify himself with the password TAKETORI and you will reply with the word TSURAYUKI. You will then hand over to him the said two parts of R 70718 loosely wrapped for immediate verification. He will give you his personal receipt and at once leave for his next secret destination.

5. The honour of the Empire is involved in this operation, and its successful outcome, as a result of the loyal and precise compliance of the officers concerned, will contribute to the approaching

triumph of our death-defying troops. A thousand victories to the Imperial land, sea and air forces.

It still needed a preamble, call signs and something to communicate my 'special operator' idea. That would have to await the verdict of Stubbs and Wallace.

Thanks to our codebreaking at Delhi we were able to quote the reference numbers of both codebooks, the old and the new. That should help to banish any remaining suspicions. I had asked Delhi if we knew the name of the signals Major at Rangoon, which would help further still. And the general suggestion that he belonged to a privileged inner circle, with its repeated injunctions to secrecy enhanced by the use of passwords, should lure him further into the trap. The first password TAKETORI was from *The Bamboo-Cutter's Tale*, a famous tenth-century story. The reply TSURAYUKI was the name of the compiler of one of the best-known anthologies of poetry, the Kokinshu, just a little earlier. Each had its own eloquently nostalgic flavour.

The jeep returned and we went out to greet Coe. Something about the way he moved belonged to the American 'walking tall' tradition rather than the stumpier progress of most Japanese. But his appearance was unmistakably Oriental, and the stereotyping was emphasised by large gold-rimmed spectacles and several gold-filled teeth. He was more smartly dressed than the rest of us, a reminder that even the US enlisted man's wardrobe was more generous than a British officer's. They handed out three or four medals to each of ours, including one for undergoing the rigours of flying training in Canada, as if they were Hannibal's elephants crossing the Alps. We swallowed our humility and gave him a warm welcome. Would he greet us, as they did in films, with "Hi, fellas"?

"Good morning, gentlemen. I understand that I have to report to Colonel Preston. Where can I find him, please?"

The accent was ninety-nine per cent authentic Californian, even if the manner was less gung-ho. We broke it to him that Preston was out, and found him a room. Henderson asked him how much he knew about our plans.

"Not a lot. I understand there's a plane to fly some place and that it's all classified Top Secret. That's all they could tell me."

"Yes and no. It's all Top Secret but there's no plane to fly." Seeing Coe's face fall he added, "So far." He described the plan and we filled in the details of the stage we had reached. Coe became more and more excited as we went on.

"You mean we're ordering them to hand over this book and they're giving it to us on a plate? What a beautiful scenario."

Taylor quizzed him. "They've promised us a 'Sally' bomber if nothing better turns up. They say you're a Navy fighter pilot. Have you flown anything heavier? Is that what those medals are for?"

Coe blinked at the forthright challenge. "Sure, but forget the medals. Uncle Sam sends them out with the rations. I trained for fighters, yes, but once I got posted to Special Ops I did a conversion course for twin-engined stuff. That Sally bomber will be very light on the controls. A bit twitchy, you know what I mean. Crew of seven. What course are we flying?"

"The first leg should be in good weather, round this big loop. If we use this different route for the return run it could be a bit bumpy."

"You mean it'll be sheer hell? OK, I get the picture. Uh, uh, I guess this will be the Colonel."

We did the introductions.

"Good morning, Colonel, sir. I'm proud to report for service."

"Join the team, Lieutenant. I'm glad to say we should have more news about that damned aircraft this afternoon. Now, how much further have we got?"

Henderson said, "Some headway, sir, but we need another round of planning. Martyn and I want to check the Japanese draft with Coe. The signals discussion is still going on. Taylor and Coe can't do much more until we get the plane, but they can swap ideas about Jap tactics and airfield procedures."

Quite unobtrusively he had emerged as a central figure in the team, an unofficial deputy to Preston. Taylor didn't look too happy; he had cast himself in that role.

"Right. Coffee next, then a good session before lunch. Send some coffee in to those two hermits."

Coe read through my draft text. "You've laid it on the line good and strong. I get the drift. This guy isn't just going to obey orders; he's going to feel proud to obey them, right? I like the psychology."

"You know more about the psychology than we do. Will he really rise to this? Is there any way we can improve the text? Is it OK linguistically?"

He pondered, stroking his jaw with his thumb.

"Nothing hits me. I'd fall for it. He'll love it. How do you encode it?"

"We'll try it on the Colonel first."

Preston smote the table with his fist and laughed a great crowing laugh. "What I most enjoy, as a lover of irony, is the bit about preventing any risk of compromising secret material, when that's exactly what the poor fellow will be doing on our behalf. He ought to be on our payroll. Excellent. Try it on Wallace next. He's got to transmit it. Then get it enciphered ready for him to take with him. You may have a rush."

Wallace and Stubbs were locked in an earnest discussion of aerials, frequencies and procedures but seemed quite happy to be interrupted. I showed them my draft.

"What's this, a magazine article?" Wallace asked suspiciously. "It's a hell of a length."

"It'll be in code, which will shorten it a bit, but we dare not shorten it much or it will lose its effect. What's the snag?"

"What's the snag?" He rolled his eyes theatrically. "The snag is that the longer it is, the easier it is for the Japs to pinpoint our damned transmitter. If they've three direction-finding sets well apart they can triangulate on to us. Even two can get a good fix. Just do me a favour – see if you can prune it, and when you encode it, pack it in as tight as you can. What's all this password stuff?"

I explained.

"It sounds a bit fanciful to me." He yawned. "Let's have a chat about the preamble when Stubbs and I have finished this session. I missed my sleep on the plane last night. That's why I can't appreciate some of these finer points."

Lunch was not a sparkling occasion. We all had our minds full of technicalities and unanswered questions, and Preston, still awaiting his signal, seemed to have run out of energy. The sultry afternoon didn't help. Someone turned on All-India radio, catching the end of an incongruous organ recital. The news summary followed:

"In Europe the wintry weather has virtually stopped military operations. In the Pacific the Japanese have withdrawn from Leyte in the Philippines. Inside India there have been further student demonstrations in Delhi and Calcutta, where police dispersed rioters with a lathi charge. There were also disturbances in Lahore and Amritsar, where lorry loads of youths chanting 'Quit India' burnt a Union Jack at the war memorial. Seven were arrested. A Congress Party spokesman claimed …"

"Turn it off," said Preston. "Lewis tells me that there was trouble in Ranchi last night, with shop windows smashed. If it gets worse we'll have to get a guard out here. We can't afford any delays. Coe, what's this about you bringing a Zero back from the Aleutians?"

"They told you that?" He seemed genuinely embarrassed. "The Japs had been raiding Dutch Harbor up there, and a stray bullet from a Catalina, of all things, cut the oil pipe on this Zero and it had to crash-land. A Navy team checked it over and I flew it back for evaluation. I guess that's all. Colonel, sir, you have a visitor."

Agnew's jeep came up the drive and he stepped across, looking pleased with himself. He offered several genteel conversational gambits, as before, but we were unresponsive. I wondered if Stubbs and Wallace ought to be brought in to any discussion, but Preston shook his head. "Let them get on with their stuff. They're working against the clock. What have you come to tell us, Agnew?"

Agnew smiled his bright little smile. "Colonel Preston, I thought it only proper to tell you and your team members that General Greatorex has given further consideration to the matters which we recently discussed."

He was still talking like a solicitor's letter but my spirits rose. Had they thought better of their objections?

"We at ALFSEA believe that the team should be commanded by an experienced senior officer. Young emergency-commissioned officers like these, drawn from various specialised branches, require the direction of a more mature officer such as Colonel Preston or myself."

Nobody said a word. There was a long silence. Henderson, whom he had not met before, was looking at him very fixedly.

"I understand that Colonel Preston may not be available to direct the operation. If that is so, ALFSEA would wish me to do so."

This time the pause was longer still. Henderson, his face flushed, cleared his throat.

"Can you enlighten us on one or two details, sir?"

"Certainly, Major, if you wish." A patient smile, humouring the new boy in the class, a dull pupil.

"I had understood that the Supreme Commander, South-East Asia, gave his blessing to this plan from the start?" Very silkily.

"In outline, yes."

I realised that Lewis was behind Agnew, impassively keeping a shortened record on his pad.

"Do I now understand that the proposal to bring in a directing officer from outside the team emanated not from his headquarters but from ALFSEA at Calcutta?"

Agnew was starting to see the drift.

"I do not see how it concerns you, but that is broadly true."

"And essentially the view at ALFSEA is that specialist officers are incapable of carrying out such an operation without the direction of a more senior officer from outside the team?" His Scottish accent was becoming ominously strong.

"Correct."

"Even though that officer has had no involvement with its detailed planning?"

"I find your remark verging on the impertinent."

"It is a question of fact, sir, not of opinion or emotion." Henderson was now pale rather than flushed, but seemed more at ease than Agnew.

"Certain qualities apart from technical expertise are called for in military matters, Major: grit, moral fibre, sense of tradition, courage in the face of danger. It takes discipline and maturity for these to develop."

"And clearly these qualities are not thought to be sufficiently evident in the present members of the team?"

"Since you force me to be blunt, no."

"In that case I propose to resign my commission with immediate effect."

Agnew was thunderstruck. "Don't be absurd."

"Far from it, sir. My colleagues and I are not specialised tradesmen in fancy uniforms. All of us underwent full military training, first in the ranks and later as officers. Most of us have been on active service in the Far East for several years – and I mean *active*." He paused suggestively. "We are now planning, as volunteers, an operation which is as hazardous as anyone could imagine. You come here and accuse us of lack of courage in the face of danger, and other moral shortcomings. If you are right we are clearly unworthy of the King's commission which we hold. If ALFSEA's view prevails I shall resign my commission at once, and before returning to the ranks will explain my reasons fully in writing to General Slim and Admiral Mountbatten, with these gentleman as witnesses. I am astounded to hear these criticisms put forward by an officer who has practically no knowledge of what the operation entails, and who comes from a rear headquarters. I say that without personal disrespect but in sharp contrast to those high military traditions you spoke of."

Agnew was furious but struggled not to show it. "If you feel it necessary to resign your commission, no matter how misguided your motives, that is your concern. The team will be reshuffled and if necessary a substitute will be found."

"What team, Colonel Agnew?" asked Taylor vehemently. "As an airman I don't come under ALFSEA. If they persist in this tomfoolery you can count me out."

I said much the same, as my unit was in India Command, quite outside ALFSEA's authority.

Preston's face was a picture. He obviously relished Agnew's discomfiture but tried not to show it. Coe too had been listening intently. His face broadened into a grin and his manner lost some of its fastidious Oriental reserve.

"Colonel Preston, sir, I need some guidance. I believe I'm an officer of an Allied power who has volunteered for temporary duty with the British?"

"Quite correct," Preston confirmed.

"That means I can pull out if I choose?"

"Certainly."

"Without being accused of cowardice by your brother officer?"

"I should hope so."

"And meanwhile I can say what I think?"

"Please do."

"In that case I want to say that I was, repeat *was*, privileged to join this mission as originally set up. I like the team and the plan they've made is a winner. All I have heard in the last few minutes is a different ball game. We have plenty of ornamental officers who come along for the ride but don't know what's going on. I thought we goofed up enough operations and you people knew something we didn't know. Whoever dreamed up this latest idea is a screwball. There's no call for me to resign Uncle Sam's commission but I'll go pack my bags."

Agnew was stunned. He could never have foreseen this unanimous refusal to serve under him, and the consequent collapse of the whole plan. He now made a bad mistake.

"I understand, then, that the gentlemen who had thought of taking part in this operation have now lost their appetite for it?"

Henderson exploded. "You'll see if we've lost our appetite. The only danger we're concerned with is the danger of being led by a simpleton who has no idea what it's all about. Back to your desk, you pallid wee man, and find something better to do than accusing us of cowardice."

Preston stood up in a hurry. "This has gone far enough. At least it has exposed a serious flaw in ALFSEA's concept of the job to be done. That has to be mended fast and it can't be mended here. Colonel Agnew will need to go back and explain that if General Greatorex persists in his policy there will be no operation to direct and no team to carry it out. I think that puts it in a nutshell, Agnew?

"Allow me to add that the reason why I am not leading the team, or what you call 'not being available', is that I have none of the relevant specialist skills that you seem to regard as a luxury or even a handicap. Meanwhile I have no orders to disband this team or to suspend planning, and I should be failing in my duty if I did so. There is a precision and urgency in this assignment which is perhaps not understood back at Calcutta. Come and see us again, Agnew, when they have meditated more creatively. Now you must forgive us; we have plenty to do."

Agnew looked as if he wanted to stand his ground – perhaps to salvage his ambitions from the junk heap – but Preston escorted him to his immaculate jeep and came straight back to us.

"Phew. Would one of you kindly get me a stiff whisky? I suggest you all join me." Taylor hurried out to take up this offer. "I don't believe I've ever known anyone threaten to resign his commission on a matter of principle before today, let alone a whole squad of officers on the verge of mutiny. I'm very touched by the solidarity of this team. There's a hint of celebration in the air, but also a whiff of a possible court martial, you realise, Henderson?"

"I apologise for my outburst, Colonel. I wonder if I should write and offer to withdraw my offensive remarks about him if he withdraws his about the whole team?"

"Hm. That might be a judicious move, but I suggest sleeping on it first. At one point I thought you were going to challenge him to a duel. 'Sir, you have called my honour in question. Choose your weapon. Mine's a machine-gun.' It will certainly give ALFSEA a headache; perhaps they deserve it." He sipped his whisky.

"But remember what I said before: Greatorex doesn't give up easily. He's an honest, sensible chap. Reliable for orthodox military matters; all at sea with the unexpected. His type were brought up to think of war as a game. I don't mean that in a playful sense; I mean it was supposed to have a set of rules like tennis or chess, which both players observed. Unfortunately the Japanese invented new rules and didn't send him a copy, and he's too hidebound to learn them. And he probably shares the view about codebreaking, even in wartime, that 'gentlemen do not read each other's mail'. Agnew is the perfect disciple. He never steps out of line, provided someone else draws it for him first. He can't even conceive that there could be surprises in a job like this. Not a trace of imagination."

Lewis bustled in. "Excuse me, sir. There's a signal coming up for you from Comilla."

"Bring the signalman over here. I'm feeling my age."

"Hello, who's that speaking? Speak up, I can't hear you. *What?* Don't shout; I'm not deaf. That's better. What's that? A frying dragon? Spell it. A flying dragon?"

Out of the corner of his eye he saw Coe give a jerk of recognition. He had to wait.

"Elephants? What is this, a nursery rhyme? Pat-a-cake, pat-a-cake, flying dragon. Are you all drunk down there? What? Yes, I know. Why couldn't you say so? Does it work? Speak up. Enunciate. *Great flaming caterpillars!* Yes, I can hear you perfectly. Where is it? When can I send the chaps over? All right. Send me a written confirmation, will you? We aren't the Department of Extinct Zoology, you know. All right, Charles. That's a wonderful bit of news. Thank you. G'bye."

The signalman looked dazed. "Don't go away. Lewis, get through to Ranchi and see how quickly you can get me a plane to Agartala for two chaps. What about those little Yankee things – L5s, are they?" Coe nodded. "Or a Lysander. Book an airship if need be. Quote the General at them. And hurry up, there's a good chap."

Lewis and the signalman moved out of earshot. Preston was in a gleeful mood.

"I wave my magic wand. Hey Preston, what happens?"

"Dragons and elephants, sir."

"Yes, you blighters. They have found us a beautiful aeroplane. Coe, you seem to know about flying dragons. Tell us all."

Coe was not accustomed to whimsical eccentrics, especially in the form of senior officers, but he rose to the occasion.

"Yes, sir, Colonel, sir. It's a newer Mitsubishi bomber. They call it Ki 67. We call it 'Peggy'."

Preston snorted. "Have your people no sense of the ridiculous? Tell us more."

"It's a twin-engined heavy bomber much the same size as Sally – I beg your pardon, much the same size as the Ki 21. We calculate it has nearly the same speed as a Zero. It has a greater range than the Ki 21. Crew of six to eight. Various gun turrets. We rank it as the best Jap bomber so far. It's the first Jap plane to have armour-plated protection for the crew, so that's good news for us. Yes sir, that sure is some airplane."

Preston, still looking pleased, said, "There's a picturesque side to the story. Apparently this one came in to land at a tiny airstrip somewhere in north Burma, overshot, and ran into a paddy field past the end of the runway. Nothing could haul it out. So my friends in Fourteenth Army moved in and rescued it for us with the help of some elephants. We'll get the full story later. Well, now it's at Agartala. I want Taylor and Coe to go down there and learn to fly it. Straight away. Can it land on Ranchi airfield? I want you and it back here as soon as possible. It's better for climate and security."

Taylor said thickly, "I think this runway's about 5,000 feet. It should be all right. But we'll have to get the feel of the plane first. Another whisky for you, sir?" demonstrating how it should be drunk.

Preston shook his head. "No, and not for you either. You get that feel as fast as you can and be back here even faster. Lewis has a shopping list of things for you to bring back with you."

Lewis came in. "We've got an L5, sir. They can just carry two passengers."

"Good man. Pick up your kit and be off with you. Tell me, Coe – why Flying Dragon?"

"It's just the Japanese name for that airplane, sir. They call it 'Hiryu'. 'Hi' is 'flying' and 'ryu' is 'dragon'. I'm sure sorry about that 'Peggy' making you mad, Colonel."

"Forget it, my friend. Off you go. Here's our shopping list. Fuel, ammunition, Jap uniforms, flying kit, insignia, oxygen masks. It's all down there waiting for you, but everything must be checked for a perfect fit. Pick up a spare radio too. And we need a lot of red and silver paint and brushes."

Coe looked pained. "We spray, sir."

"Very good, you pedants. A plentiful supply of sprays and a Master-Sergeant with a PhD in spraying. Now beat it."

Their departure reminded me that there was still no news of our general-purpose man. I asked him how we stood.

"You're right to remind me. I suspect the RAF have gone to sleep over it. Bring back that signalman and we'll put a bomb under their personnel people. Tell him to get me the Air Officer Commanding or his deputy." He hummed idly and played a tune on the table with his fingers.

"Is that you, Dick? Look, we urgently need a man for our special mission. He'll have to be a volunteer. First and foremost he's a good radio-operator. Then he's an air-gunner, perhaps a navigator and with luck a reserve pilot. I asked your personnel people and what happens? Damn all. What's that? I know it's a tall order. But what about all those chaps who flew small planes solo before the war? They did their own navigation and radio and usually the maintenance as well. I don't care if they have up-to-date RAF certification for all that stuff as long as they know it basically. What about the fellows who flew for Burmah Oil? The ones I knew are all greybeards by now, or I'd have recruited my own. All right, Dick, I know you've other fish to fry. Can't you pass this to your Number Two and tell him it's the General's special job? No – I can't tell you why on this line, but it would make your hair stand on end. Thanks. G'bye."

"If I know the AOC's office we could hear within the hour. What's this, a deputation?" Wallace and Stubbs had emerged from their long discussion. He summarised the meeting with Agnew, Henderson's bombshell and the reaction of the rest of the team.

"Sorry to have missed the fun," Wallace remarked, "but I do believe we've solved your signals conundrum at last. Can we try it on you?"

"Go and fetch Henderson and we'll be the jury. That's better. Go ahead."

Stubbs started, looking relaxed, his stutter hardly noticeable.

"One. Our bogus signal has to seem to come from Singapore. That's the only place with an HQ that m-might plausibly send this signal to Rangoon.

"Two. The operator must be dropped in Malaya. That's the only place our signal can be sent from without inviting the Japs to pick up the discrepancy in direction.

"Three. Therefore the signal preamble must say it's from Singapore, otherwise the Rangoon operator will smell a rat if he's in cahoots with the direction-finding units. But the real Singapore operator will also be listening in on the same frequency, so we invent a bogus 'special operator in Singapore'. His name happens to be Wallace, and he won't be in Singapore, but we won't tell them that.

"Four. He will come in 'under the net' as we call it. His radio will be tuned before he leaves Colombo, so that it has the same note as the big Singapore transmitter. That's not logically necessary, because ours will turn out to have a separate operator, but we think that psychologically it m-may help to reduce surprise or suspicion."

He coaxed his recalcitrant pipe into smouldering steadily, and leaned back. Wallace took over.

"Five. As soon as we've settled in, we eavesdrop on their morning midday schedule. When that finishes we jump in and use the ordinary operators' jargon to say: 'Sorry to prolong the schedule. Here is an urgent signal for your CO, marked "For his eyes alone", relayed by Singapore Tokushu Joho Bu, or whatever Martyn calls it, on behalf of Imperial HQ. Message begins …', and then we rattle it off. That should explain why it's a fist they don't recognise, and give them a cosy 'special secret' feeling. If they have heard of TJB it will strike the right note, and if not it will sound more important and mysterious still. That's the atmosphere Martyn wants for the message itself, and we think that preamble will reinforce it."

Preston smiled like a Cheshire cat. "Go on."

"Six. At present the message tells the Major that he must be the only person to see the message, which is a self-contradiction because his cipher clerk will already have deciphered and read it, secrets and passwords and all. So immediately after the heading 'Most Secret' the text will run: 'For the eyes of the CO, Signals Section … blah, blah, blah … only.' At that point it is the clerk's duty to jump up, call his CO and let him do the rest of the deciphering himself. That's highly unusual, so again it should have the right spy story flavour."

Preston smote his brow. "To think I took you for a bunch of amateurs. It's delicious. Chocolate nut sundae with Grand Marnier. Go on."

"Seven. With a secret signal like this, people don't just tell the recipient to destroy it after reading; they insist on a destruction certificate. We think that should go in the signal, and the Major should be told to hand the certificate to our General Whatsisname.

"Eight. It will take about twenty minutes to transmit this signal, and we think that fetching the Major, perhaps from his lunch, and giving him time to decipher and decode it, could take one or even two hours more. Remember he'll be out of practice. So if we aim at about lunchtime for our transmission, we should give him a choice of several times for his confirmation to us; we suggest the 1700, 1800 and 1900 hrs schedules, so he has a choice and doesn't feel flustered. We want him to be our flattered and punctilious friend. Fortunately Malaya and Burma are in the same Japanese time zone.

"Nine. We make it easy for him to confirm personally, without further flimflam, by telling him to send the clear group 4343 at one of these times, which we in turn will acknowledge with 9898. That will heighten the atmosphere still more.

"Ten ..."

"What!" cried the Colonel with all the pathos of a ham actor. "Will the line stretch out to the crack of doom? Another yet? Proceed."

"Ten ... and the last, sir. As soon as we get his confirmation we change our frequency and tell Colombo that he's swallowed the bait – or at least pretended to – and that will be in a different fist, for greater security."

"Excellent. Has anyone the slightest qualms or any sort of amendment?"

"A small one," I put in. "The Japanese believe that ascending numbers are lucky, so could we make it 1234 and 6789 instead of 4343 and 9898. That'll give him a more comfortable feeling."

"By all means let's give him his lucky numbers. Anything else? Then remembering that Stubbs is off tonight and Wallace soon after, I must congratulate you both on those plans. They take the 1944 prize for ingenuity."

"One thing I hadn't mentioned", said Wallace, "is that Colombo are planning to drop a pair of us. That's the normal pattern now. My partner, Lee Kim San, is a first-class young Chinese born in Singapore. He's a really good radio-operator and will have his own radio, which is a useful standby, but he doesn't know anything about these extras. How much can I tell him?"

"Hm. You know the rules. You mean that if you came a cropper in the drop, he would simply take over and send our signal just as you would have done?"

"I do. And obviously I must tell him before we leave."

"In that case you must have absolute discretion. I can't authorise it, but if we wait to clear it through the Supremo you may hear too late. So you can take it that the answer is yes, though I didn't tell you and you didn't hear me. Is that quite clear?"

"Yes, sir; thank you. The other thing is that I hope you can let me go back tonight. There's a tight schedule because we are starting from scratch. We have to cancel all our previous plans, agree on a fresh dropping zone, find out about local contacts, wait for the weather, do the jump, set up the radio, get your signal off – all before you can fly to Rangoon. And the signal isn't ready yet."

Preston thought briefly, then agreed. "We'll put you on that night plane and the signal will be ready to take with you. How long will it take, Martyn?"

"I'll do it straight away, sir. It's largely a question of adding the new points and checking the rest."

"That reminds me. We need a cover name for this operation. There's a choice of three. It all started with your idea, so you can have first pick: Kangaroo, Paperchase or Buffalo?"

"Paperchase chooses itself, doesn't it?"

I included the extras we had agreed on: the signal destruction certificate, the method and times for confirmation, and so forth. Then at the start we had the formula:

MOST SECRET

FOR THE EYES OF THE COMMANDING OFFICER, SIGNALS SECTION, 5 AIR DIVISION HEADQUARTERS ONLY. URGENT

MESSAGE RELAYED BY SINGAPORE TOKUSHU JOHO UNIT
ON BEHALF OF IMPERIAL HEADQUARTERS.

That would give Major X something to think about, because
such a preamble was without precedent. Then I coded and reci-
phered the code groups for the new details, and checked the whole
thing yet again. I doubt if any signal has ever been checked so carefully – but after all we had the honour of Japanese Imperial HQ to
sustain. We were still at the mercy of Wallace at the friendly end and
Major X's operator at the other.

I handed the whole lot over to Wallace. There were two copies,
for him and for his colleague, Lee, both on rice-paper which can
be eaten very quickly if necessary, though we should all have been
disappointed, to put it mildly, if our efforts were to pass down the
gullet and into limbo before the signal had been sent.

Stubbs came out to join us for a drink before dinner. He was
thinking morosely about going back into Burma in a few hours'
time. He knew, and felt deeply, that the rest of us were likely to
be in the team and he would not. But the whole question was in a
tangle – who would lead the team, who would be in it, and where
did Agnew fit in?

"Adur," said Preston over coffee, "is that jungly snake-charmer
still living down at Patratu?"

Adur darted his tongue between his crooked teeth, adding to
the saurian image. "I t'ink so, Colonel sahib. You want we bring him
here?"

Preston glanced round at us. "You agree? I think we've earned
a little relaxation. Lewis, you take Adur and find him if you can. We
paid him twelve chips last time, so you won't have to bargain for
long."

He and Henderson had seen it before, but the rest of us hadn't.
"How do they learn the trade?" Stubbs asked. "It seems a risky business until you're an expert."

"It's a hereditary job. It goes from father to son for umpteen
generations. No women snake-charmers that I know of, unless

Cleopatra was one, the serpent of old Nile. They think it started in Egypt. I've seen it done in Afghanistan too, when I was …"

"Excuse me, sir," said the signalman from the doorway. "Your reply from the AOC's office."

"Thank God for that. Good evening, Dick. You have? Wonderful. I don't care if he's an Eskimo; this outfit's like the Tower of Babel already – as long as he'll fit in. He's a volunteer? Can you send him up here – no, on second thoughts would you put him into Agartala with our two lads on the Flying Dragon? Yes, thank you. You're a great man. Sleep well.

"With luck we've got a complete team, gentleman. That's our Jack-of-all-trades, a Dutchman, currently a Flying Officer in the RAF at Calcutta. Flew small planes all round the East Indies and Malaya before the war. He's now retrained to fly heavier stuff and has brushed up his radio technique. He'll do. I wonder how soon they can get that plane up here. I don't want them down in that hellhole near Calcutta. It gives me the creeps."

The snake-charmer was a wizened Moslem, with bare feet and a many-coloured pagri, who slid noiselessly into the room with Lewis and Adur. He and Preston exchanged salaams, and Preston asked him in Urdu how he and his wives were getting on.

"They are treating me so terribly, Colonel sahib. There is no peace for the wicked or the good. Always they are wanting money, clothes, jewels. Please be careful, gentlemen. Is not so good British feeling in Ranchi today."

He squatted on the floor and began unwrapping a great cloth bundle, layer inside layer.

"You see, this man is a specialist. No soapstone models of the Taj Mahal to sell. No wooden boxes allegedly carved by the virgin daughters of Kashmiri princes. Simply a snake-charmer."

The bundle was now much smaller. Out of one yellowish cloth he brought a cobra, very docile and somnolent.

"Don't be frightening, please. I take out the poison."

From a dingy blue cloth he produced a musical instrument like an oboe with a swollen waist. He blew with pursed cheeks, and a curious sound filled the room – nasal but rounded, like a drowsy bumblebee. He moved his fingers on the holes and a slow mournful melody emerged. It quickened, and the cobra moved a little.

The tune rose, grew and jumped. The snake followed, still very placidly. It began to uncoil and stretched upwards. He pushed it gently down on the cloths and pulled out another cobra. Soon both of them were slowly swaying to and fro. I noticed that he used the glass-blowers' technique of breathing in through the nose while still blowing out uninterruptedly through the instrument.

I don't know if the snakes were hypnotised, but I was. The music droned on and on, the snakes waved from side to side and from time to time were bedded down again. I think he provoked them into striking once or twice, to remind us how dangerous they might have been, but the scene sticks in my memory like a hazy dream, quite detached from time though it probably lasted no more than half an hour.

At last he finished, wrapped the cobras up in the bundle of cloths and made a quick bow to us. Preston's word 'jungly' was too harsh. The man was an artist, despite the jumbled cottons to clothe himself and house the snakes.

Stubbs and Wallace went back in the jeep with him, to catch their night flights back to Calcutta and Colombo. They had guided us through the signals labyrinth where one false step could wreck the plan and cost us our lives. Stubbs would be back in the muddy chaos of the Assam-Burma border. Wallace was now the vital link in the chain that would shortly launch first the signal and then us at the unsuspecting Major X at Rangoon. He had the risky job of parachuting into enemy-held territory and staying there. However acute the dangers of our trip might be, they would be over in a few hours. His might last for as many years.

"I wish you good journeys and happy landings," Preston said. "And please give appropriate greetings to your Chinese colleague,

Wallace. Good luck." Lewis drove them, the snake-charmer and his snakes down the lane.

It was a starry night with a thin sliver of moon. There was a murmur of voices from the servants' quarters, and some cheerful noises still rose from the village, but the massive stillness was almost unbroken. The haunting pavane of the snakes kept running through my head. We stood on the verandah and drank it in. Preston mused, "Uncanny, isn't it. There are wars going on in both directions and we can't hear a thing. You could forget they are slogging it out in Europe. What time is it there?"

"Early evening," Henderson thought. "My wife will just be starting night shift. She's applied to come out here as they are short of photo-interpreters, but the mills of Whitehall grind slowly."

"Taylor's wife wants to do the same, but the Home Office grinds even slower than the War Office. If Slim's plans go well and the Yanks keep leapfrogging across the Pacific, it may not be worth their coming out. I give the war in Europe another six months. This one could be over in twelve or so. Give the bureaucrats their heads and they could still be sitting on those forms when it ends." He stretched. "Anyway, I'm turning in. There's a long day tomorrow."

He trundled off happily. We watched the moon rise further and decided to follow his example.

DAY FOUR:
ALARMS AND EXCURSIONS

"Good morning, gentlemen," Preston said to Henderson, Lewis and me at breakfast. "We seem to be strangely depleted. Did you get them packed off last night?"

The self-effacing Lewis gave one of his rare and rewarding smiles. "It was a treat to see them, sir, all three. Captain Wallace was so excited that he almost forgot to take his parachute and radio with him. Captain Stubbs was cool and collected and I had to run after him with his wallet and pipe. The snake-charmer was very quiet and didn't lose any snakes at all. Very fine officer-like qualities, that man. Grit, gristle, breeding, moral fibre, sense of tradition, courage in the face of danger …"

"Disgraceful remarks, Lewis, grossly prejudicial to good order and military discipline, but showing great discernment. To keep you all up to date: Mountbatten has ruled that there is no objection to our scheme on signals security grounds, nor to our using a Jap plane if we can find one, as we now have. So that knocks two of the planks out of Agnew's platform, though he won't find out at once. Mountbatten doesn't yet know about the leadership row. He'll go berserk when he does.

"I promised to keep you posted on that subject. Lewis has just typed out my rough draft of a letter to Agnew. Will you both read it carefully? It's deliberately high-flown and long-winded. I don't think he'd appreciate everyday language. I'll send it in a day or two, when he thinks he's got clear away with his machinations, but I want your frankest comments first. Meanwhile I've got a plaguy telephone call to make."

The letter ran:

My Dear Agnew

When General Greatorex decided to propose changes in the leadership of the team which is under my personal direction, he did not communicate with me in any of the usual ways. He chose instead to use you as a messenger, bringing not a letter but an oral message, as on your earlier visit.

You arrived without warning and chose to speak to my team as soon as you saw them, without having told me who the message was from or what it was about, although part of it concerned me personally. You did not even, as an officer junior to me, ask my permission before addressing them. In your haste you did not notice that two of the team's members were missing – on special assignment – although you had met one of them the previous day. You also overlooked the presence of my NCO assistant, to his embarrassment. All that I find very surprising.

It is stranger still that Allied Land Forces, South-East Asia, at whose headquarters I believe you are employed, appear not to have grasped the fact that three of the four officers who were present are serving in India Command, the RAF and the US Naval Air Force, and therefore fall outside their remit. The remaining officer, of field rank, immediately proposed to resign his commission in protest at ALFSEA's high-handed intervention and your own unfortunate comments. None of this augurs well for the operation.

Henderson shifted uneasily. I had already noticed that he looked as if he had hardly slept. Surely he hadn't regretted his outburst? All he said was, "Agnew will think a ton of bricks has fallen on him."

When I reflect also that ALFSEA's help is not required with any aspect of the proposed operation, that they cannot yet have any specific understanding of its nature or purpose, and above all that you yourself have neither knowledge of nor interest in its details, I am astounded. On this point perhaps I should remind you that the reason for my not being in charge of the operation itself is that I judge that I have insufficient specialised experience. I am not convinced that the appointment of someone with none at all is the answer.

I think you will agree that I am usually the last man to stand on ceremony. This, however, is a matter of common courtesy, or perhaps of uncommon discourtesy. When an officer or a gentleman disregards the norms of military or civil behaviour he cannot expect the matter to escape notice. When that person has been so censorious about the character of others, the contrast is acute. The fact that your involvement and personal advancement were being canvassed is hardly an excuse.

I heard Preston's voice in the distance, raised in anger. His telephone call must be going badly.

Sgt Lewis's presence may, as it happens, prove a happy accident in case there is any dispute over the actual words used. He is an accomplished shorthand writer and has a standing instruction from me to note verbatim all discussions relating to the operation. He was thus able to keep a complete record of the occasion. I feel sure you will agree that this could prove convenient ...

"Miaow, miaow," I thought.

... but it will of course be destroyed as soon as the matter is closed. In case any objection may be raised on the grounds of his NCO status, I am glad to assure you that he has several times been recommended for a commission, and when he feels freer to take this up I have no doubt that he will make an excellent officer. As to his technical competence, I think you will find that the officers in this team will testify – as I do – to the accuracy with which he has recorded their remarks. He also has TOP SECRET security clearance.

I greatly regret that you have obliged me to raise this distasteful subject, and I trust that you will refrain from any repetition. I shall then be spared the painful necessity of protesting more formally through General Slim and Admiral Mountbatten, under whom I have the honour to serve.

Yours sincerely,
Michael Preston

He came back, looking outraged, while we were discussing this remarkable letter.

"No, it's not Agnew again. Just a bunch of idiots who need their heads banged together. I can't tell you the details yet. Perhaps they will climb down. Now, say frankly if I've overstated the case to Agnew."

Henderson said carefully, "My only doubt is about the sheer length. Is the bit about Lewis all necessary?"

"Logically no, but psychologically yes, I think. It's not that relevant, but Agnew is a man who worries more about having a button undone, or talking carelessly in front of the servants – social solecisms of any sort – than about really important issues. That's why I put in all the NCO details. He'll be quite old-maidish about that, so I clouted him with it. I simply want to eliminate his interference for these few crucial days. That should come under the heading of fair means, not foul. You see the point? Anything omitted? Hardly? If he bowls googlies at me he mustn't complain if I try to hit them for six.

"Now, I've found out what the snake-wallah meant about 'not-so-good British feeling'. Apparently an Army truck knocked down a Hindu holy man, a Saddhu, in Ranchi yesterday. He died on the way to hospital. The driver is in the guardroom on a charge, but the local Congress Party are demanding that he should be tried before the local Indian magistrate. Just what we could have done without, whatever the facts are. To be on the safe side I've arranged for some old Gurkha friends to mount guard down the lane and patrol round the house. I'll also take Adur and his suave assistant on one side and threaten them with terrible retribution if they utter so much as a squeak about what we are up to – not that I fancy they can have the foggiest idea.

"Further afield, in Burma we have recaptured Kalewa and put two bridgeheads across the upper Chindwin," – Henderson whistled – "so things are moving. That sets the scene for an advance towards the Irrawaddy and makes our Operation Paperchase all the more urgent. So the last titbit is very timely: Taylor and Coe have just completed their first full test flight, taking turn and turn about as pilots, and are quite happy about the way it handles. The Dutchman has just arrived there too, and now all three are going to practise circuits and bumps with a full load on board. They plan to fly here before dusk.

"Let's see. It's about 400 miles; at about 250 m.p.h. that makes less than two hours. Lewis, get on to Ranchi and make sure they are expecting them. My God – warn them and everyone in the area to be kind to a plane with Jap markings on that run. I expect the AOC has remembered it, but it's not on the usual list.

"I want VIP treatment for that machine and the crew. Don't forget the Dutchman; nobody knows him, not even his name. Get Ranchi to tell us when they are due, and we'll go over and roll out the red carpet ourselves." He went off as cheerful as a schoolboy.

Henderson suggested that it was time to start polishing up our spoken Japanese for use at Mingaladon, and we could stretch our legs at the same time. We walked up through the wood and across the heath, but he was clearly thinking about something else. Eventually he came to the point. "I'd like to consult you on a personal matter. I know I can count on your discretion. Just before I came here I had this appalling letter. What do you make of it?" He pulled out an airmail envelope and gave it to me. Inside was a single flimsy sheet of plain paper.

DEAR SIR

THE WRITER REGRETS BRINGING YOU BAD NEWS BUT CONSIDERS IT HIS DUTY TO INFORM YOU THAT YOUR WIFE IS BEING UNFAITHFUL TO YOU. SHE IS CARRYING ON WITH A FOREIGNER AND HAS BEEN SEEN WITH HIM TOO CLOSELY TO BE MISTAKEN

A FRIEND

The capitals were written in a stilted and rather uneducated hand, with several corrections. There was a London postmark on the envelope.

I was horrified. What would I feel if I had a letter like that – if I had a wife? Everyone knew that London was brim-full of charming Polish and French servicemen, all claiming to be bachelors with titles and rich estates at home. More recently the Americans with their casual and generous *bonhomie* had arrived in force, and it was notorious that their private soldier was paid more than a British lieutenant. The half-serious comment was 'Overpaid, over-sexed and over here.'

But did the letter ring true? I read it again, more carefully.

"A genuine friend would put his name to it, however reluctant he was to give you bad news, rather than torment you with an anonymous letter. The vocabulary doesn't sound convincing; all those mealy-mouthed words. With those poison pen clichés it could be from anyone."

"My first instinct was that it was a hoax from someone who hated my guts. But be honest – should I take it seriously?" He looked desperately anxious.

"My reaction is the same. We know the place is full of eligible foreigners, but why doesn't he say which nationality, or even give a name? The bit about 'his duty' can cover 'her duty'. Surely poison pens are traditionally frigid and repressed women bent on making mischief? I suppose an unfulfilled bachelor, or even a youngster who's read about these letters in the popular press, is just as likely. At all events I can't see a wife of yours running around with Yanks and Poles or anyone else."

"Nor me, thank the Lord. She's the last person I'd suspect, and if she were unfaithful, as the writer tastefully puts it, she'd be the first to tell me."

"Then my advice is to burn the thing and put it out of your mind, apart from the nasty taste. It doesn't even prove malice against you personally. I suspect that a warped person would get the same thrill out of messing up the life of a complete stranger. Burn the thing."

"Nothing I'll enjoy more. Adur was surprised when I borrowed his matches. He thought I was taking up smoking."

The flame was invisible in the dazzling sunshine, but the paper turned purple, then black. He dropped what was left, stamped the ash hard into the ground, and drew a long breath.

"Why didn't you ask Preston? He's the complete man of the world."

"I nearly did, but I preferred someone nearer my age. Besides, you and I have met before this particular picnic. But he's an extraordinary chap, isn't he? I can't see myself signing on for this trip with anyone else in charge. Yon wee scunner Agnew, for example. Did you ever meet anyone so perjinkety in your life?"

He saw my baffled face and put on his broadest music hall Scots accent. "Hoots, mon, ye dinna ken the wurrd? Perjinkety is pernickety. Finical. Prim. You Sassenachs are starved for words. Now it's time to do our Japanese roles. I'm cast as the General, so will you be their signals Major? The password is TAKETORI."

"My password is TSURAYUKI, sir."

"Hand me the codebooks, Major."

"I regret that the codebooks are not immediately available, General."

"Have you not fully understood the instructions? I can give you one minute and no more ... Major, I will give you exactly thirty seconds more. If no codebook and no explanation is forthcoming, you will be instantly shot. Colonel Miyaguchi, cover Major X. Twenty seconds, ten seconds, bang." I agree, it's tricky. Is there any better ploy?"

"What about 'I believe the instructions from Imperial HQ are quite clear. Unless the codebook is produced instantly I shall have no choice but to place you under immediate arrest and report your gross dereliction of duty with a view to summary court-martial'?"

"Either will do if he has no book with him. I agree that the second's better. Shooting won't help and will bring the locals in before we can get clear. Suppose he has the book but needs some coaxing? Shall we entice him into the plane? We open the door and say, 'Major, come on board so that we can set your mind at rest.' You agree?"

"What about an extra bait? 'Major, come on board. I wish to discuss another subject which may concern you personally." He'd find that hard to disobey. The moment he's inside we knock him on the head and take off at top speed."

"Suppose he has the book but refuses to come on board?"

"For Pete's sake, this is getting worse all the time. Hit him on the head, grab the book, pull him into the plane and run. If he's out of reach we shoot, not to kill, and grab him and book just the same. Anything to delay their finding out what has happened."

We had stumbled on one thing: we couldn't just assume that the handing-over would be easy. There were countless variations on the theme, and the team would have to be practised and ready for anything.

There was a distant clatter of firing in some field exercise, and intermittent thumps where tanks or artillery had a practice range. And it was time for lunch.

"There's one other thing," he said. "Before we land we make sure the coast is clear. We can't make conversation with Major X, whom I'm getting to like, if we find truckloads of infantry making for us at full tilt. We simply take off with our tail between our legs. So as soon as we land there, we must run back to the head of the runway, ready for a quick getaway."

"Agreed."

We descended, still jabbering Japanese. He had a rich vocabulary and a fine command of the myriad verb forms, which convey varied flavours and subtle implications. With his example I was starting to remember or relearn some of them. He had also mastered typical Japanese voice production better than any other non-Japanese that I have known. With his acting experience and good linguistic instincts he had convincingly absorbed the breathy and throaty drawls that punctuate Japanese speech, and he uttered them authentically like a ventriloquist's doll, his lips and teeth hardly moving.

"What are you two up to?" asked Preston as we approached. He was fanning himself with a folded sheet of paper.

"We are being Japanese officers, sir, and thinking up as many unpleasant surprises as we can."

"Don't joke about unpleasant surprises. I've just had a most disagreeable signal. It'll keep till the others get back. Meanwhile we are overdue for lunch and Adur is giving me a dirty look. I wish I could say the same for his acolyte, Smiley Boy. Adur, my friend, we are ready."

After lunch, expecting that there would be a long evening's work, we strolled across the fields, taking the signalman with us in case of news of the plane. He had a No. 48 set, heavy but allegedly portable. My sense of foreboding was suddenly strong. Preston and Lewis, and perhaps all the rest, were old hands and wouldn't suffer from first-night nerves, but I found myself wondering again if we would be flying into a death trap. Nobody had played down the dangers. Preston had gone out of his way to voice them starkly. But was there a risk that our excitement and optimism, in pleasant surroundings and with good colleagues, could still blind us to them? How could they be honestly assessed? Wasn't it more rational to back out and leave the whole affair to really brave men? To the professionals? After all, it hardly needed me to identify a codebook. But now it looked as if a professional, of a sort, was likely to be imposed on us as leader, and this, far from improving our chances, might well ruin them. And what if, meanwhile, the Japanese started using the new codebook?

The time dragged by, and we returned to the house. Preston consulted his watch. "1600 hours. It gets dark about 1830, at least as a deadline for landing an unfamiliar plane on an unfamiliar airfield. We should be hearing soon. But they could be sitting on the end of the Agartala runway banging a gauge to see if it's playing tricks or not."

A pair of Gurkhas were now guarding the bottom of the track and another pair came past the house. "I've warned them not to terrorise Adur and Co.," Preston said. He watched the third pair sauntering along the bottom of the field and chuckled. "You know about the Colonel's lady in Delhi who explained to newcomers from England that Gurkha officers were white but had coloured privates?"

1630 came and went. We mooched about dispiritedly, killing time. Henderson was writing a letter; I thought I could guess who to. 1700. A motorcyclist came roaring up the track and ran to Preston.

"Sir, your plane is halfway here. The radio link seems to have gone bust. We kept trying …"

"Never mind, man. Thank you for coming over. *Lewis!*"

Lewis was already climbing into the jeep.

"Quick, climb in and hold on. It's only seven miles."

It was rough track at first, but soon we were on the metalled road and racing along smoothly in the cooler air. At the airfield Lewis took us up a side turning, bypassing the guardroom and finishing at the HQ building. "Speaks volumes for *their* security," said Preston, who went ahead, then reappeared and beckoned us over. We went up on to the flat roof, with the control tower one storey above us. 1730, 1745. Various birds of prey, angular and menacing, hung and dived over the nearby fields. A gang of labourers was still digging out the foundations for an extension Indian-style, with one man wielding the spade while another helped by tugging a rope attached to it. "And if I lived on their rations I should be doing the same," Preston commented. 1800, and the runway lights came on. It wasn't dark, but the distant lights began to fade and shimmer. 1815, 1830.

A Flight-Sergeant called down from the tower. "They're only just down the road, sir, coming over Ramgarh any moment."

A few minutes later we heard the unusual throb of their engines and saw their navigation lights sweeping round to the north, then north-west, then turning and coming lower. They did a long slow run with flaps down and landing lights on, obviously having a good look at the runway before landing. As it roared overhead we could see that someone had sensibly painted a blue ring outside the red roundels to prevent mistakes.

It flew off in a big slow circle as before. Then it disappeared, and for a few anxious moments we wondered what had happened. It came in sight again, low and almost hovering as seen from our foreshortened view, and floated downwards in the gathering dusk. There were several firm bumps and it came rolling fast down the runway, slowing down with brakes squealing.

"Damned good." Preston had been on edge like me. "I confess I was flying it for them with the pit of my stomach, although I'm no pilot."

The plane turned and came lolloping over the rough grass, turned and stopped, guided by an RAF batman. They revved the engines briefly, then cut them. The navigation lights went out and a hatch opened under the plane, nearly reaching the ground. Henderson clutched my elbow. "See that? It looks as if there's no side door. Allow for that in our plan for dealing with Major X."

Three figures clambered out stiffly. First Taylor, podgier still in flying gear; then Coe, sparer beside him; then a much shorter man. Preston greeted Taylor and Coe briefly and turned to the third.

"Piet Buisman, Colonel, at your service." 'Colonel' was in three syllables. He saluted.

"Welcome, my friend. You've all done remarkably well. What's to be done with this plane overnight?"

"We'd like it towed to a hangar, locked up and well guarded. We just need to get our kit out, then we can kiss it goodnight. Would you mind giving the orders for that, sir? We'll show you round tomorrow, if you like."

Preston went briefly into the HQ and returned. "That's fixed. Where's Lewis? We'll need a second jeep."

Lewis, without being missed, had already got hold of a staff car and a driver. "Ask no questions. I mentioned the General's name and they fell into my open hands."

We split up for the return journey, Buisman with Preston in Lewis's jeep and the rest of us in the staff car, a plush affair. It was now dark, and our headlights shone yellow on the rough contours of the road. We turned up our track past the Gurkha guards, who gave crashing salutes. A disconsolate signalman was waiting for us. He stepped forward.

"I'm sorry I let you down, sir. I must have used up the battery without realising it. It's as dead as a doornail. It's my fault that Ranchi couldn't contact us."

"Don't take it to heart, lad. I shan't put you on a charge. Go down to Ranchi to put a new life in your set, and be back first thing in the morning. Carrying that thing will be your punishment. But don't do it again. Understood?"

"Yes, sir. Thank you very much, sir." And he went off, a man reprieved.

"He'll cadge a lift anyway," Preston soberly observed. "Adur, can you give us half an hour before dinner?"

"Ji han, sahib. All will be quite correct."

A little later, above the splashes and snorts, I heard Preston singing in his bath. It was part of the Fauré Requiem, where the men chant 'Agnus Dei, qui tollis', yet something was wrong with the words. I tiptoed to the door. Sure enough, he had altered the text to 'Agnew Deum se credit' – 'Agnew thinks he is God.'

There was just time for me to wash and change and we were ready to sit down. Buisman, out of his flying kit, was revealed as a swarthy, wiry little man with raven-black hair and pronounced crows-feet at the corners of his eyes. Preston, having taken his revenge on Agnew through his private musical joke, was in his most expansive mood. "Buisman, you are the newest arrival so you will be on my right. The rest of you, sort yourselves out." He then, without warning, said a two-word grace, and we all sat down.

"Would you mind to tell me, Colonel, what was that thing you said?" Buisman asked.

"I said, 'Benedictus benedicat': may the blessed one bless us. Nobody seems to have noticed that it's Sunday, and it's apt for an international banquet like this."

"Nostalgia. That's what it did for me," Coe remarked. "I was raised at a Catholic college and they said grace every meal. Went on to seminary and they said it all day. You know I wanted to be a priest? I was dead set on joining the Catholic mission to Japan, converting my heathen brothers to be Christians. Instead of redeeming them for heaven we're bombing them to eternity. Now the Americans have killed my grandparents when they bombed Tokyo. And I'm one of the Americans. The whole world's crazy."

Buisman frowned at Coe. "And when the Americans bomb Eindhoven they kill my brother and my sister by mistake. How could they do that when the Germans couldn't do it? I tell you this to be frank, not to make trouble. It's the first time I fly with an American. It isn't comfortable for me. Nothing personal against you."

Preston interposed. "Adur, where's that food?"

The three who had brought the plane back looked worn out after their long day. I felt unaccountably shivery and sluggish. Preston said, "Tell us something about your background, Buisman. You are a man of mystery."

"I can solve that, sir. I am thirty-five years, Dutch citizen, born near Bandung in a little place called Tjiumbuleuit. My father ran a travel agency, my mother died when I was a little boy. I got a job with Royal Dutch Shell to fly those little planes to take people to an oil well or pick up machinery, so I settle at Palembang where they have a big depot. I marry a Dutch girl who has been stewardess on 'Oranje', and we have two little childs. When the war start I join the Dutch Air Force. When the Japs come they put my wife and both girls in a camp in Sumatra and I don't see them these nearly three years. Just no news at all.

"So if you ask me if I am volunteer I say yes please. I have flown all around and I know Burma quite a lot. I will make any role what you want. I have trained for pilot and I can work a radio and shoot a gun. I have a good knife if I need it. I am fit, I do every day gymnastic. They tell me about your scheme. I think it is damn crazy to risk five men to collect a book, but I cooperate. I do anything what you want to fight the Japs."

There was a pause.

"We shall be very glad of your services," said Preston, "and I welcome you to the team. Now," – he sensed that Buisman wanted to go on – "who's going to tell me the story of how we got hold of this plane? I've only heard the headlines so far."

"I'll start," Taylor announced. "Tell me if I leave anything out."

"There's a tiny Jap airstrip at a place called Singkaling Kamti, in the upper Chindwin valley, north-east of Kohima, right up in the wilds." I could see Preston mouthing 'There's a little green-eyed idol to the north of Katmandu' but he didn't interrupt. "Apparently our chaps have been keeping an eye on it for some time, using the local Kachin tribesmen as scouts. They reported that the place was only held by a small Jap detachment. Last week the bomber landed there. It skidded off the runway on to some marshy ground and got stuck. After getting several other things stuck too in the process of trying to pull it out, the Japs gave up. Sixteen Brigade decided the time was ripe to take over. They sent in two columns with Kachin guides. The first went east from Kohima, over the mountains between two ten-thousand-foot peaks, down a ravine, and blocked the track to stop Jap reinforcements coming from Homalin."

He ground his cigarette out.

"The other column came over another high pass fifty miles further north. When it was ready the RAF put in an attack to keep the Japs' heads down, and we took the airstrip. They had strict orders to keep the plane intact. I don't often say nice things about the army," smiling disarmingly, "but they did a good job there. They brought in Williams and his elephants and a team of six of them hauled the plane back first go. They've got a photograph, elephants and all, yanking the thing out with long chains."

"I've never met Elephant Bill Williams," Preston reflected, "but I've seen those Burmese elephants and they are very wise. They train them from earliest days and give them a young lad of the same age who stays with his own animal for life. They only use them for really heavy work after they're twenty-five. By then they can lift one ton or pull two. Go on."

"Then they flew in an RAF flying crew and mechanics. They checked it over and found nothing wrong, so they filled up, towed it to the other end of the runway, ran up the engines, said a few prayers and let go. They say it slewed to and fro but they got it out of the valley and brought it over the top to Agartala."

"I take off my hat to those boys," said Coe, "getting it out of a hole like that when they hadn't flown one before."

"You're right. There were some nice touches, too. They knew that the Japs mustn't miss it, so as it took off they sent three Beaufighters along the valley, just above it, to drown the noise and confuse anyone watching. And you remember that Sally bomber we were interested in, before this turned up? They flew that in and dumped it in the same place. It flew well enough for that. They're both Mitsubishis and look much the same on a quick recce."

Preston asked, "And you're happy about the condition ours is in, and using it for our mission?"

Taylor nodded lazily. "Fine," Coe said. "I don't say I love it, but it handles easily, even full up. I guess the worst thing is the noise. This one rattles like a birdcage, but it's solid enough. The first thing I propose we should do, Colonel, sir, is to take a trip with all the party on board, so we can get used to it and work out some details of the operation. I suggest we do that tomorrow morning. Just flying practice, not combat practice."

Taylor nodded again. There seemed to be less friction between those two now that they had something to do.

"Well, you lot did a good job getting it here and we've certainly no time to waste, so that's agreed. I've two things to announce. There's an order from our garrison commander. In view of the local unrest you are to carry revolvers at all times. A damned nuisance, but make sure you comply. Lewis will draw one from stores for anybody without." Coe looked amazed. "I want that sorted out before you go to bed, and you will be properly equipped from breakfast tomorrow. That's an order, whatever you think of it. Understood?

"There's also some unwelcome news that concerns us more closely. This signal came from Fourteen Army HQ this morning: 'GREATOREX INSISTS OPERATION PAPERCHASE PERMISSIBLE ONLY IF AGNEW IN COMMAND AND HENDERSON WITHDRAWN STOP SUPREMO STILL

IN WASHINGTON STOP MEANWHILE CONTINUE PREPARATIONS STOP COMMENTS QUERY SLIM'.

"You know my thoughts. I am past being mortified. The officer in question knows Burma like the back of his hand, at least to the extent of the Maymyo golf course. He speaks Burmese fluently enough to order a gin and tonic. How useful those gifts would be when confronted with a reluctant Japanese officer I cannot surmise. He's courageous enough, possibly foolhardy; it's just that a poodle-faker is the wrong man for the job. Lewis, you heard nothing of that. And there's absolutely no question of removing Henderson.

"I'll get on to Vinegar Joe Stilwell, who is deputy Supremo while Mountbatten's away. He's a curious ally, but Slim gets on all right with him and he's an enemy of red tape and other stultifying conventions, so there's hope. No resignations will be accepted by me while we await a ruling from SEAC. Business as usual. Let me assure you that I have known far worse crises than this, and they have all come right in the end, even with less powerful allies than we have. So no long faces. Meanwhile I'll make sure that Colonel Agnew recognises the importance of coming on tomorrow's trial run, so that he can learn the ropes and get to know the hypothetical members of the suppositional team of which he may be presumptive leader." I caught Lewis's eye; he winked.

"Lewis, get him on the line, will you? We need to have him here for breakfast with us, while we mull over our plans. Remember that he won't have had my letter yet, so no naughty remarks. Henderson, will you brief Buisman on that business? And Taylor and Coe need bringing up to date. I must have a word with Adur about a proper breakfast for the occasion."

The whole plan was now a complicated balancing trick. Everything had to be completely ready and if possible foolproof. We had to allow for setbacks in training or a delay to the operation because of bad weather over Malaya or Burma or both. But these preparations and precautions took time which we could not afford. The new codebook might come in at a few hours' notice, and then it would be too late. No bogus message using the old book would stand a chance of fooling them then.

Fortunately all the evidence was that the various obstructions that ALFSEA had placed in Preston's path had not put him off his stride. He seemed not to suffer from nerves, and he was balancing the factors – signals, crypto, flying, human, logistic – without apparent effort, like a skilled juggler keeping five balls in the air whilst walking a tightrope and humming happily. His bluff manner – that of a buffoon in a French farce – deceived nobody for long.

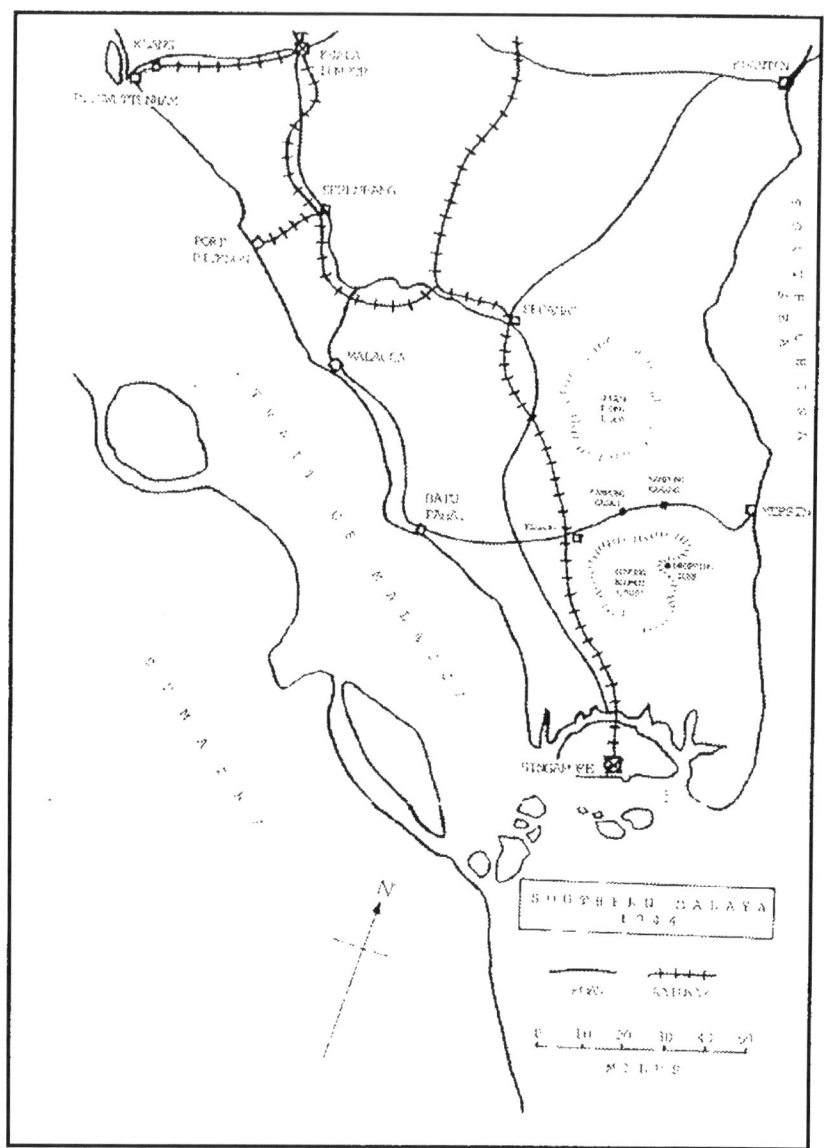

Map of Southern Malaya 1944

WALLACE TELLS HIS STORY: I

Lee Kim San was waiting for me at Colombo airfield and it was good to see him again. During my brief stay at Ranchi I had come to like and trust the team there, but it had been a diversion, just as sending their weird message would be a chancy and irrelevant episode for Lee and me at the start of an assignment that might last several years. And I resented having it dumped on our plate at the last minute.

We drove to Force 136 HQ, which ran our undercover activities in Malaya and Burma – the most useful ones, anyway – ordered cool drinks and compared notes.

Lee was about thirty, with a wide, sleepy, slightly pock-marked face, strong glasses and unlimited energy. He was the son of a Chinese businessman in Singapore who had been running a thriving import agency before the war. Lee had travelled widely in his father's business, specialising in selling cameras and film, and he was experienced and dependable. Even as a student he was interested in local politics, and when the Sino-Japanese war broke out in 1937 he helped with the China Relief Fund, which brought him into contact with the Malayan Communist Party. I don't think he ever joined, because their policy of boycotting Japanese imports would have meant a clash with his father's business interests, but he had many friends both there and in the 'Anti-Enemy Back-Up Society' which intensified the boycott and dealt with those who infringed it.

All this could have led to trouble with the authorities, but when Germany attacked the Soviet Union the MCP's policy switched to include full support for Russia and her allies – including Britain.

That is why the main organised resistance to the Japanese in Malaya after Singapore fell came from the Chinese. The Malays, Indians and Tamils were often helpful in various ways, but they were more easily cowed and their commitment was personal rather than racial.

So the Chinese community chose some of their brightest young men to train for resistance groups in case the Japanese invaded Malaya, and Lee was on the first course. Unfortunately it assembled only after the invasion had begun, because the British authorities were so complacent and dilatory. As the head of Special Operations Executive in London, the parent of Force 136, blisteringly put it, "It is most tantalising to see how His Majesty's Representatives have vetoed any preliminary work, cried for help from SOE the moment trouble began, and then complained if we did not deliver the goods."

In the end Lee was lucky to get out of Singapore before it fell, finally reaching Ceylon via Sumatra; his parents stayed behind. He was sent on training courses on firearms, explosives and radio, and excelled as a radio-operator. He spent six months with the joint Chinese-American force in south China and north-east Burma, which gave him valuable experience, and he had been picked for several earlier drops into Malaya, all of which had been cancelled for one reason or another. I explained that we were now saddled with an extra chore before we could get down to our proper work, and that the change of area meant abandoning all our painstakingly contrived preparations and working against the clock on new plans, starting from scratch. Lee took this calmly, without the sense of grievance that I felt. For him it was just another challenge, and he was impatient to get on with it.

One urgent task was to get our drop put at the top of the queue: my job. Another was to collect every possible crumb of information about our part of Johore: Lee's job, and a much tougher one. And we both had to make sure that our personal preparations were complete.

Most of them had been complete for weeks. There was our survival kit: a body-belt with Malayan currency, a really good compass, revolver, ammunition and knife and – curious articles for 'survival' – the 'L' (for lethal) tablets for suicide that were supposed to act instantly and must always be accessible. No easy matter. We had also borrowed items from the RAF escapers' kit: a compass hidden inside an unscrewing jacket button (with a left-hand thread to fox the opposition) and a silk handkerchief that was normally khaki but could be turned inside out to reveal a map of Malaya. We would be wearing warm waterproof clothes; Malayan mountains can be the coldest and wettest places in south-east Asia. To these we added other maps, cipher tables, frequency lists, schedule times, and the special signal for the Ranchi mob, all on rice paper, instantly chewable.

I rang South-East Asia Command at Kandy and found that although they had received Preston's signal stressing the change of drop to Johore, local inertia had still to be overcome in the shape of those who had already booked it for Pahang and were reluctant to change: the familiar deskbound bureaucrats in uniform. We sidestepped this obstacle by sending a signal by the Great Circle Route: asking Preston to ask Slim to ask Mountbatten to bulldoze any obstruction. Overnight one wave of his magic wand transformed the ogres into good fairies who fell over themselves to be helpful. They were Mountbatten's Bright Young Things, generally known as 'The Dicky Birds' since he was often referred to as 'dicky' – even as 'Tricky Dicky'. Fortunately the detailed planning was done by people who were just as enthusiastic and rather more reliable. As soon as the present heavy clouds over Malaya cleared, they promised us, our mission would be flown. We were Number One on the list.

The change from Pahang was more than a psychological jolt, it was a flaming nuisance. I had spent most of my dozen years in Pahang, knew large areas well – especially off the beaten track – spoke the local dialects passably and had many contacts. For me Johore was simply Singapore's home county that we passed through by train. Luckily Lee knew it fairly well, and it wasn't difficult to choose the best general area for our DZ (dropping zone). The Japanese were known to keep mainly to the roads, patrolling them often by day and occasionally by night, usually in large parties. So our guerrilla bands kept to forests and mountains much of the time, and crossed roads only by night and with great caution. We needed to be dropped close to those mountains, and we picked out two areas from which we could send the bogus signal: Gunung Blumut, about fifty miles north-north-west of Singapore, and Gunung Tiong, some forty miles further away.* 'Gunung' is Malay for mountain, and these were both sprawling mountain masses over 3,000 feet high, and well placed for later raids on the main railway line from Singapore.

Lee would be going in with me, but as soon as we had sent the signal and made contact with the locals we would split up, working with resistance groups some fifty miles apart, and trying to get them to coordinate and intensify their activities against the Japanese instead of feuding between themselves.

There was little reliable information about either the Japs or the guerrillas in these areas. An awkward feature of the Communist hierarchy that controlled the guerrillas was their 'divide and rule' policy. Lateral contact between adjoining groups was discouraged and even local initiative within a group was frowned on. This lack of enterprise wasted the talents of their brighter subordinates and boosted the position of yes-men. Moreover the central organisers, mostly excellent men, were overworked through having to tour this very difficult terrain on foot, handing out directives one by one to each unit – directives that might be out of date. While they were away from HQ, urgent decisions had to be delayed. Nobody else had authority to make them, and nobody would risk assuming responsibility.

So Lee and I had to trust to luck in choosing our DZ. Gunung Tiong scored in sheer remoteness, and thus in freedom from Jap interference, but we could not find out which of the tracks shown on our maps were still passable. Unless they were constantly cleared by chopping down obstructions, these tracks became overgrown within months, and no map or report existed that could give an up-to-date picture. Having already spent several years hacking my

* see map on page 78.

82

way through virgin jungle, I decided on Gunung Blumut. There had been a report some months earlier of an active guerrilla group in the area, and the local Sakai tribesmen were believed to be less timid and secretive than elsewhere. We needed their help in shifting the heavier loads that we were taking in.

Lee was quite happy about dropping there. Before the war he had regularly visited Kluang, a small town nearby, where he hoped some former customers might give him help and reliable news. There might be more Japs than on G. Tiong, but the chance of better tracks clinched it. The Japs were a lesser evil than really impenetrable jungle.

We got our HQ to send a message to the local guerrilla group by a roundabout route, saying that two of us were coming soon and asking them to look out for us. We had no great faith that the grapevine would deliver this in time, but at least it had never yet betrayed our intentions to the enemy.

The snag about having no real contacts was that we should have to guess at a detailed DZ and do a blind drop. That meant no friendly torch signals to identify the best spot and show that it was safe from immediate Japanese interference, and nobody to help recover the loads, hide the parachutes and carry the stuff to safety during those first vulnerable minutes. Moreover east Johore lay outside the range of photo-reconnaissance aircraft, so we had to content ourselves with small-scale pre-war maps. We narrowed the choice down to a small valley running north-east from the central peak. Tin mines, paddy fields and rubber plantations might have changed its complexion since the maps were compiled but the contours must be the same. We would have to trust to luck and make a snap decision.

At present there was a full moon. How much longer would it serve? How soon would the weather clear? Here Fate had dealt us a trump card. The codebreakers' out-station at Bangalore had recently broken the Japanese meteorological code. Now, by courtesy of the enemy, we had daily weather reports on Malaya from Singapore; one copy came to Force 136 HQ by teleprinter about breakfast time.

Another daily event was physical training, to lessen the risk of injury on landing and to prepare us for mountaineering with heavy loads. We practised our Malay and the local Chinese dialects, Cantonese and Hakka. And we polished up our Morse, both the Allied form from Colombo traffic and the Japanese version used by the Singapore and Rangoon operators. We could pick up their signals easily, and it was a bizarre thought that the same men might well be on duty when we broke into their network.

We checked the stuff to be dropped with us: seven loads. Medical stores; concentrated rations; weapons and ammunition; plastic explosive and detonators; a radio each; enough books to keep us sane when the tropical rains made movement impossible for days on end. We made our umpteenth pleas for the parachutes *not* to be white. That showed up too clearly and could give us away the moment we landed. Everything was in balanced loads. Ever since the debacle of the Norwegian campaign, when the ship with all the ammunition had been sunk, rendering useless the undamaged ship with all the guns, this had become a belated principle of packing – yet another masterpiece, I thought savagely, of wooden-headedness on the part of some staff officer which ten seconds' thought by an intelligent amateur would have exposed.

At HQ there were files bulging with intelligence reports. For Johore they were scanty. Vague rumours and isolated names cropped up in shadowy patterns, with a worryingly large amount of optimistic conjecture.

Then Lee came back from Colombo Public Library proudly carrying a compendious book by the Reverend Matthew Coningsby: *With Camera and Canoe in Malaya: a Butterfly-Hunter's Memoirs*, published in 1903. He, like me, had been attracted by their variety – but what was Lee grinning at? "Try the Johore section." It was brief, but page 143 held two sepia photographs with Gunung Blumut in the background. One showed the real shape clearly: a bluff peak, wide tumbling foothills and ravines carrying turbulent streams which, the author said, sometimes became cascades. All of this rang true.

Whatever had happened to G. Blumut since, this pattern decided our DZ – right up by those slopes.

We took our book, maps and ideas down to Negombo and showed them to the pilot who had been briefed for our flight, a lanky Queenslander, lean-faced and lantern-jawed, laconic and a trifle mulish. No Pommy bastard was going to teach him his job. Bill Garrett soon learnt that we simply wanted to pick his brains. He didn't like blind drops, chosen off a map with no local contact. Fuel got used up. There was never any to spare, so there was no spare time over the DZ either. That meant bringing the bloody parachutist back again and another bloody trip. Pardon my Spanish. More danger of Jap fighters if you went back to the same bloody place.

"There's my cobber, Jake. He's my co-pilot. He knows a trick or two."

Jake had an even stronger Aussie twang. "Hair abairt the claird?" 'Claird' was the big query. No problem for most of the flight, but near the DZ you had to come down through the cloud belt. If there was a mountain in the way, Christ. Our plan looked OK but it needed bloody good flying and bonzer navigation. Otherwise it would be a oneway trip. We agreed that G. Tiong was a reserve DZ if G. Blumut was overcast. Either way the fuel would be almost gone when they got back, so the main leg would go across Sumatra instead of detouring down the Malacca Strait to avoid it.

"Holy cow, they've got so many problems I don't reckon they've got many planes in Sumatra now. If we go over real high they'll never hear us. We save a hatful of fuel. You realise it takes nine or ten hours each way, non-stop? If we fly faster because we're scared of falling asleep, then the bloody fuel runs out faster and we don't make it home. We might get better weather tomorrow. I doubt it."

There was a message waiting for us at Colombo. A submarine had just docked at Trincomalee, bringing back another stay-behind man. Did we want to meet him? We made the trip to the north-east in record time. He turned out to be Stephen Callander, whom I had heard of but never met. Because of his intensive course of anti-malarial mepacrine he was almost as green as his bush-jacket, and even seedier-looking than I had been. His reports cheered us up, on balance.

The Japs had pulled their better troops out of Malaya to reinforce Burma and Indo-China. Those left behind were less active than before, but they were just as fanatical in a fight. He had seen Liberators flying low, even in daylight, without being attacked. Any suggestions? Double your medicine, get better jungle boots, take sharper tools to hack through jungle, take any delicacies that you especially crave, to keep up morale. And apply for a safe job in a pleasant area, rather than this blankety-blank mission.

We rang up HQ to see if there was any chance of our flight next day. "Doubtful," they thought, "but just possible. Ring back at midnight." We knew it would leave about 1500 and we were all packed up, so we made a leisurely journey back and dined at the Galle Face Hotel where, it was said, diners once found reassuring notices at each table: 'All water served here has been passed by the Manager.' Afterwards we sat back and talked about the extraordinary phenomenon of the overseas Chinese.

Their success started because the native peoples of Malaya and the East Indies, though competent farmers and small shop-owners, are mainly content with an easy life and don't look ahead overmuch. Why should they, when a paddy field can give several rice crops a year? The Chinese, however, are planners, hustlers and go-getters. When they emigrated they set up banking and trading links, much as the Jews did in Europe, and like them they established tight family and community links. Their word was their bond. If anyone broke it he disgraced not just himself and his family but even his Chinese competitors.

Above all, they planned ahead. None of the Malays' easy-going 'sufficient unto the day' philosophy. If they made a penny a day they were in business. They saved the pennies – which the Malays would have spent happily – banked or invested them profitably, and after a lifetime's modest living and hard work they retired in comfort. All the family worked in the business, which often stayed open round the clock. Promising youngsters were educated and trained, if necessary with help from the community, for the communal good. They now held a virtual trading and banking monopoly in south-east Asia. They were often resented, but they had become essential for its prosperity.

A strange thing about the guerrilla groups was that they often didn't apply this logic to military matters. Sometimes this was because some sectional or linguistic difference got in the way. Perhaps it sprang from their national pastime, gambling. Instead of planning an attack carefully and sticking to the plan, they would trust to luck, bravery and improvisation, and that made them a sitting target for the Japanese. Little of this was true of the younger, better-educated élite. Lee was as resourceful and reliable a colleague as anyone could have wished for.

At midnight we rang again. The chances were even, they said, so stand by and ring after breakfast. Then the message was, "The weather looks better but one of the engines is playing up. They are stripping it down and by midday it should be ready to test. Bring your kit and have lunch here." This stop–go pattern is so much part of service life that we weren't greatly bothered. It always gets sorted out in the end.

The airfield at Negombo, on the west coast of Ceylon just north of Colombo, is beautifully placed among waving palm trees and vivid green paddy fields. Any breeze from the sea can keep it fresh, but without the breeze it becomes a steamy swamp. We were lucky. At the HQ building we met Helen, the WAAF officer who arranged these flights for Force 136.

She had a gift for steering her clients deftly into a good mood. Most suffered from butterflies in the stomach whether they admitted it or not. Some were quiet and morose, others garrulous or argumentative. Some talked happily about anything unconnected with their mission. Others wanted to check the last few details again and again, sorely trying the patience of the ground crew, who could sympathise up to a point, and of the flying crew, who had plenty to preoccupy them already. A few, having seen no European women for several years, became flirtatious. With these she dealt firmly but with good-humoured tact, so that feathers remained unruffled.

With her high cheekbones and wide-apart eyes she could almost have passed for Chinese until you saw her hair – dark brown, not jet black. Cool and efficient as usual, she said, "You hear that noise? That's your engine being tested. Unless something goes wrong in the next ten minutes, the flight's on. Come and have lunch."

The mess building looked across a lawn to the trees, and the long windows let the breeze drift through the dining room. We ate well, knowing that there would be only snacks during the flight, followed by hectic activity after our drop. Then we took ourselves and our kit across to the aircraft. The ground crew confirmed that the flight was on, and that the loads to be dropped with us were already on board. We checked them against our list: seven, each with its own parachute. "And we got you your fancy chutes in jungle green. Don't blame us if you can't find them. At least the Japs won't."

We put on our flying kit and immediately felt suffocated in the blazing afternoon sunshine. Once airborne and after sunset we should need it, but Negombo was not the place for it. We waved goodbye to Helen and the ground crew, the big doors were shut and we settled ourselves in the surprisingly comfortable canvas seats.

Bill Garrett came down the vast fuselage, much of it filled with extra fuel tanks. "Welcome to K for Kangaroo. Make yourselves at home, what there is of it. Don't worry about that crook engine; she's OK really. No smoking *at all*, remember. She's full to the brim with fuel and it'll be a long bumpy take-off run." There were the usual preliminaries and then we used every yard of the long runway. At last we were up, the coastal plain dropped away, we had brief glimpses of the sharp central peaks, and Ceylon dwindled below and behind us.

The first few hours were uneventful. From our height the Indian Ocean was formless and almost cloudless. The continuous drone of the four big engines became a blur at the back of the mind. The Liberator was a very large plane for its day, and the feeling of space and solidity was welcome after my hedge-hopping trip from Ranchi in what the pilot had affectionately called a 'flying perambulator'.

Lee and I played cards. Being Chinese he won almost every round, even when I introduced him to Slippery Anne. He had the Chinese habit, disconcerting to newcomers, of unwittingly providing a background of clicks to every activity by pulling his double-jointed fingers lengthwise to keep them supple. Jake came back with coffee and a surprisingly good hot meal in stacking cans. He chatted amiably about his family and their home near Brisbane, and we exchanged guesses on how long the Far Eastern war would last. He went forward again and we dozed intermittently as the sun began setting behind us. Some time later he came through on the intercom. "We're near the Sumatra coast and Bill's taking her up to our ceiling. If you need more oxygen or more heat, turn the knobs up one click. OK?" Soon we saw an island to our right and a hazy grey coast ahead, with blue-green mountains running up steeply.

"Look out for an island inside a lake," said the intercom. "It's called Lake Toba. The Bataks down there are cannibals so we're staying well up." The light was steadily fading but we could just pick out the lake, surrounded by high, forest-covered peaks and with a large island taking up most of the centre. The plane droned on with only a minor air pocket or isolated pinpoint of light to break the monotony. There was a wide stretch of flat east Sumatra to cover, and an equally featureless crossing of the Malacca Staits.

"Wake up, old-timers." The intercom suddenly came to life. "Malayan coast ahead. Not much detail yet. The first lights to port are fishing craft, and the next lot are the coast at Batu Pahat. Oxygen off, please. Come forward to see the world."

We were on the last lap. Our eardrums and the changed engine note showed that we were freewheeling down, losing height and speed. The moon was on our right with patchy clouds around and below it. We swung north-east and followed the valley up to Kluang, crossing the railway and passing several thousand feet above Lee's sleeping pre-war customers. The dispatcher, who doubled as radio-operator, helped us into our parachute harnesses, checking that they were tight and couldn't slip. A shadowy mass loomed closer below us and the big plane began to heave and jolt.

"That's the foothills of your other mountain. Don't worry."

We flew on and circled slowly to our right.

"Now look out to starboard and look hard."

The patchy moonlight just showed the valley road, with faint lights in the villages but no sign of traffic. Paddy fields and plantations flashed by in no clear pattern. Had we overshot our DZ?

"My controls, Jake. Help them to spy out the land."

"Your controls. By cripey, what's up?" The plane had lurched horribly as Bill swung it hard round.

He said something picturesque in Queenslandish, then, "A ruddy great chunk of mountain. We nearly collected some to take home to Aussie. Who drew that bloody map?"

We circled again, finding what looked like our DZ area vaguely lit through gaps in the cloud, but confused in the shadows.

"That looks all right."

There were gentle slopes, terraced into rice fields. With the moon behind us we couldn't see if they were wet or dry. Never mind. There was a good area of them and they were sloping more steeply now, so the mountain must be close. We had to make a quick decision. "Let's go."

"Good luck, cobbers," said Bill. "Get back to the slide and we'll drop the loads as soon as we see your torch."

The slide, still a novelty in the Far East, made it easier for us to drop close together. The dispatcher checked that our static lines were clipped on the roof cable and sat us on the slide, Lee immediately behind me. The ground, now alarmingly close, raced past and then turned on its side as the big plane banked away from the mountain.

"Remember the drill? The second the red light turns green, down you go."

The minute that passed while we turned and ran in again seemed to go on for ever. Then the red light came on, followed quickly by the green. Before I realised it I had let go and was out in an explosive current of air, and suddenly the harness jerked hard on my shoulders and I saw the parachute wide open above me. I had a few moments to enjoy the sensation. Then the ground came up, much too fast, and I prepared for my forward roll. It began with a startling thud and ended with a squelch as I fell sideways. I was on the bank of a small irrigation ditch. My right arm felt numb.

I collapsed my parachute and freed the harness, then ran across to direct the rest of the drop away from the ditch. The first field was dry, thank God, and I saw Lee running towards me. The plane had already turned and I waved my torch frantically. Nothing happened. They flew overhead, banked again, came in slower and much lower, and suddenly seven blobs shot out in quick succession, each parachute opening precisely in turn and the last falling so close that I had to skip backwards to avoid it. A beautiful drop. The plane banked again, winked its navigation lights once, and disappeared over the peak.

Lee came across. "All right, Sam?"

"Except for a damaged arm. Let's clear these loads up."

We got our breath back, focused on the dark terraces and picked our way towards them, finding the parachutes one by one and carrying the loads back to a dry corner. Suddenly there were four loud explosions from the far side of the mountain. I had reached instinctively for my revolver before I recalled that Bill had promised a diversion. Perhaps he had attacked the railway to account for his low flying.

Unfortunately my right arm was much stiffer. I must have sprained something badly in my clumsy arrival. But we got the loads together and folded the parachutes into a single bundle which we could drag well away from the danger area. Our eyes were now better attuned to the jumble of light and dark patches, and we could see that we were on the edge of the small valley, further up than we could have dared to hope. Only a few hundred yards away the trees began and the foothills sloped upwards. Our first job was to cover our tracks and get ourselves and our loads under cover before dawn.

I was able to sling our stores on my left shoulder, leaving Lee with more than his fair share. After a couple of hours all the loads were under the trees and we had even repaired the worst of the damage we had caused to the rice terraces. The Malay labourers would notice, all right, but with luck they would keep it to themselves, especially now that things were going badly for the Japanese.

We sat on our bales and considered our next moves while we drank hot soup from the thermos. We had to move higher up. If at the same time we worked across the nearest shoulder of mountain, covering our tracks, we could reduce the risk of being found. The snag was the big loads; until we got help we had to hump these ourselves. First we had to explore.

We made our way up the slopes. So-called 'impenetrable' jungle is usually negotiable with care and patience, and we were lucky. The ground was strewn with dampish dead leaves, so we could move quietly. There were vines and creepers festooned round and between the trunks but they were no great obstacle. The trees themselves rose sheer for over a hundred feet. Their tops disappeared in the shadows. It was like tiptoeing in carpet slippers through a medieval cathedral.

The difference lay in the noise. As darkness falls the chorus of frogs and grasshoppers wakes up, and soon there is an incessant medley of grunts, squeaks, honks, rattles, whirrings and chirrupings. We had been well used to this, but during our stay in Ceylon we had forgotten it. Now that we were virtually new arrivals we found it deafening. Midges and mosquitoes hummed round us – a reminder that they would be biting us through the night.

After half an hour we found a small stream and followed it uphill. We entered a narrow ravine with a clutter of rocks above, and climbing past these we found a hollow that would serve as our first cache. We spent the next hours ferrying the loads up, each taking longer than the one before, until all were dumped. We covered them with rocks and buried the parachutes deep at the bottom of the ravine among some thick tree roots. We knew of too many teams that had come to grief through skimping these tiresome chores.

It was too dark for Lee to tell what was wrong with my arm. It felt as if I had broken my wrist and dislocated my elbow at the same time. We both needed a good night's rest, and as I was clearly not going to get to sleep with this pain, he gave me a shot of morphine. Then we bivouacked in the growing light and slept, clothes, boots and all, with our tommy-guns beside us. We had arrived.

DAY FIVE:
TRIAL RUN

The signalman, duly chastened, had returned from Ranchi when we met for breakfast, and Agnew had arrived in his jeep. Preston acted the host well, given the underlying tension.

"I've ordered a curry because we shan't get much lunch. No problem for old hands like you and me, Agnew. These youngsters may find themselves outclassed."

Agnew didn't look enraptured but could hardly decline. He said little and kept his distance at one end of the table, from which Lewis had been tactfully banished. Henderson placed himself at the other. The meal was a formidable affair, with plenty of side dishes. Taylor demolished an enormous plateful, but I still felt too dopey to eat much. What was wrong with me? Was it just nerves?

"Now let's think this out. You are suggesting that we do a practice flight and nothing more, leaving the Rangoon arrival techniques to be worked on later?"

Taylor and Coe were agreed. "Yes, sir. What we learn about the layout of the aircraft may decide what those techniques ought to be. Take one example: this plane hasn't got the usual side door – only a hatch underneath where anyone boarding is out of sight and we can't cover him with a gun." That confirmed what Henderson had spotted at once. "We'll fix a route that will be plain sailing while everyone gets his air legs and finds his way round. Then we'll do some bumpier flying through clouds and we'll throw the plane around a bit. It's no use if everyone is airsick when we touch down at Mingaladon. There are plenty of sick bags."

"Any questions? Any comments, Agnew? Very well. We'll get over to the airfield and talk to the met people. I've sent for a truck and Lewis has gone ahead. Collect any personal gear you want. Adur, you will look after our things very carefully indeed."

"I watch him good, sahib."

At the airfield they had pulled the plane out. By daylight it looked almost graceful despite its menacing armament and unfamiliar camouflage. We went upstairs to flying control. The met officer was on the phone, jotting down details of wind strength and direction which his clerk transformed into symbols stuck on the big wall map. He put the phone down.

"Keep well away from north Burma today, Colonel, unless you have urgent business there. The worst of the monsoon is supposed to be over but it's having several last flings this year. There is cumulonimbus up to 60,000 feet, which is twice as high as you can go, and it stretches down to nought feet. So you can't go over or under. Don't try going through. Last month we lost a Liberator in it. A bloody great Lib. They don't build them stronger than that. It didn't hit a mountain. It just broke up in mid-air."

"Who was flying that Lib?" Coe asked anxiously.

"I don't remember their names but it was an American crew and they knew that route well. They were flying supplies over the Hump to Vinegar Joe's men at Kunming and they'd only done a quarter of the flight."

If the Liberator was particularly sturdy and the Flying Dragon particularly lightweight, perhaps this was the time to pull out. Find some excuses – plead what Oscar Wilde called 'a subsequent engagement'. Had the same thought struck the others? Hard to tell from their faces. Agnew looked thoughtful but still said nothing. I noticed that Taylor was not throwing his weight about so much. His manner towards Preston was almost obsequious, and apart from some bickering with Coe and waspish remarks to Buisman, he was fitting in better. He was now recommending a course up the Ganges valley towards Delhi, our recent flight in reverse.

"I'm no spoilsport," said Preston. "If you people want to see the Taj Mahal I've no objection to seeing it again."

"Forgive me, sir," Taylor said. "I'd no idea you were coming."

"*Not coming?* Of course I'm coming, and so are Colonel Agnew and Sergeant Lewis. Did you seriously think I was going to stand here waving goodbye?"

"I'm delighted, sir. I guessed wrong."

"You shall make amends. What's our ceiling?"

"It's supposed to be around 30,000 feet, sir. We'll soon find out. We need oxygen practice for everyone anyway."

"Then if we go to Delhi and turn sharp right, whatever you people call it, we can go past Naini Tal and up towards Nanda Devi, where I did some climbing in the thirties. Didn't reach the top, mind you. That's 25,000 feet, and if it isn't bumpy enough for your purposes, God bless my soul, you can go on until it is."

Taylor and the met officer studied the map. The route was free of cloud and they could keep us posted by radio if it clouded over.

"That reminds me," Taylor said. "There's a Jap radio on board but we want to fit an extra one. Could that be done when we get back? A night shift, if need be?" He looked at Preston hopefully.

"Can do," said our RAF colleagues. The General's top priority was becoming famous.

"And please put out a reminder that we're friendly despite the funny markings."

We walked across the tarmac. Coe went to do his visual check, and soon the engines were running. Taylor climbed in with some difficulty and brought down armfuls of Japanese flying kit. "We've brought a wide range of them. Would you try these for size, Colonel?"

Preston looked like a grizzly bear; the helmet and oxygen mask made him more like a Martian. Agnew chose a set and dressed fastidiously. He looked preoccupied, perhaps because we were rehearsing an operation that he knew so little about. Or was it that he sensed the team's hostility?

Everything had been cleaned but the cut of the clothes was strange and the insignia struck a jarring note.

There was a sudden silence when Coe cut the engines. He and Taylor showed us how to worm our way through the narrow hatch with its built-in steps under the plane. There was a lot of grunting, though Preston was remarkably agile for a big middle-aged man. Agnew looked pallid as he sat down, and I felt stifled.

It was a really surprising contraption. The fuselage was long and would have been roomy, but there were few places to stand upright. If you weren't careful you cracked your head on the roof-frames. The main-spar of the wing crossed through at knee level, and other projections included three large fuel tanks, the empty bomb bay with its complex mechanism, the butts of machine-guns, a rack of oxygen bottles and the lower part of the cannon turret. The thin metal skin was held on very slender ribs, and the control wires working the rudder and tail simply ran through slits in these ribs. It looked fragile and makeshift.

"Quite normal," Coe assured us. "You get no trim on fighting airplanes. Even Flying Forts and Libs are just the same."

We found places where we could plug in for oxygen, intercom and flying-suit heaters, under Coe's guidance. Buisman swung himself nimbly into the turret. Henderson sat on the padded hump for the radio-operator, just behind the cockpit, while Lewis and I crawled back towards the tail turret, which promised a good view but threatened excommunication. Preston settled himself massively on the floor, with Agnew nearby. No words passed between them.

"All correct, sir?" asked the ground-crew Sergeant. He swung the hatch up with a thud. Buisman came down to lock it, murmured, "I wish you happy landing, sir," to Preston, and clambered up again, moving easily. I felt stuffy and clumsy in this ape-like costume.

The radio crackled as the pilots talked to the control tower and the ground crew. Then the port engine, after some laborious grinding, burst into life with a roar and a cloud of oil smoke, and after rattling a good deal settled down to a steadier note. Then the starboard engine. Coe gave a thumbs-up sign to wave away the starter trolley and chocks, Taylor revved both engines up and we began to move, bumping over the sparse turf and setting the grass quivering in the slipstream until we reached the tarmac, then rolling ponderously along the perimeter track to the main runway. Wherever the concrete sections joined, all three wheels jolted awkwardly.

The plane swung round to face straight down the runway. Each engine was run up in turn, and the control surfaces were swung to check that they moved freely. The flaps slid halfway down. A green light winked from the control tower, both engines rose to a higher note, Taylor released the brakes and we began to gather speed. A series of thuds, then the tailwheel came off the ground and the ride became less jittery. A lighter bump, then another, and we were airborne. The ground dropped away, the wheels came grinding up and locked in place with a thump. The port wing dropped and we circled, climbing steadily. The airfield was a blur lost among the jumbled browns, greys and greens of Bihar. Then there was that ominous drop in the engine note which suggests engine failure but is only the airscrew moving to fine pitch. The flaps came right up and we climbed more slowly. It was nearly 0900 hrs.

At first the view below showed the rolling hills, then it merged into the vast Ganges plain, with a kaleidoscope of emerald paddy fields from which the sun glinted, some drier fields in a paler green, an irregular pattern of roads and railways, a rash of villages, and the occasional town sprawling along both banks. Benares and Allahabad slid past. Far over to our right the foothills rose sharply towards the Himalayas and disappeared into clouds. Preston looked disappointed.

Coe came back, neatly dodging the obstructions, and tapped Buisman on the foot. They conversed in shouts, and Buisman went forward to the cockpit. Coe explained, "We're still figuring out the switches for the intercom. They're not labelled. Then it'll be easier to keep in touch."

Taylor motioned Buisman to the co-pilot's seat and he took over, running through all the manoeuvres: climbing and diving, banking, changing speed, adjusting the flaps, and then flying normally. After all, he had been flying longer than the other two and would quickly pick up the feel of a new plane. He came back and shouted in Preston's ear, "They tell me to say that we are going up to Naini Tal. That is your favourite place?" Preston nodded happily and thumped one gloved hand inside the other.

The intercom spluttered into life: "We've sorted out the switches. We're going higher. Flying-suit heaters and oxygen on, please. Coe will check with you." It was an odd sensation at first, but I realised that my breathing had become laboured and was now easier. Before long the suit gave some welcome heat.

We passed to the north of Agra, with the Taj Mahal more commonplace in daylight but still handsome in its setting of dark cypress trees, and flew north across the valley. It was already narrower and its floor rose more steeply. Paddy fields gave way to rough heath and then to low hills. Small rivers fed by hillside streams ran crookedly down. The villages became more compact. Fir and pine woods covered the slopes. The roads were fewer and zigzagged down the valley sides.

As we climbed, we began to lurch more in the air pockets. Preston was staring out of the starboard window, getting his bearings. Then he called me across and shouted in my ear, "That's Naini Tal, the lake with hills all round. You know it, Agnew?"

Agnew gave a non-committal grunt and didn't look out.

"The big hill's Tonnochy. I used to walk up there and back before breakfast – or even run, if none of the pukka sahibs was watching. Are the dinghies out on the lake?"

They were. Lucky people on leave or the few that had retired there, were sailing thousands of feet below us, possibly wondering – if they had any wits to spare – what an aircraft was doing so far off the beaten track. The pilots did Preston proud. We circled outside the ring of the hills, high enough to see the lake all the time, before turning north again.

"Turn the oxygen up one notch." Preston went on pointing. "Hill stations all round here. Almora down there, Ranikhet over the other side. Now, let's see if we're in luck. Look as far forward as you can."

There was a shallow layer of cloud above the foothills but nothing to be seen in the distance. Yet he seemed to be looking *above* the cloud, well up in the sky. Was he hoping to see eagles or lammergeiers? Suddenly I focused on the whole mountain range, impossibly high above the clouds: a line of jagged white peaks, brilliant in the sun and in stark relief against the distant haze. Preston gave a running commentary.

"Nanda Kot on the right. Nanda Devi to its left. The long ridge is East Trisul with Trisul peak at the far end. All well over 22,000 feet. Still seventy miles away, though you may find that hard to believe. Was it worth coming?"

We kept climbing as we drew closer, and it was much bumpier as we flew over the hidden foothills. That extraordinary jumble of needles, buttresses, precipices and glaciers dominated the view and became clearer all the time. It was literally difficult to believe our eyes, which showed this immense array of rock, snow and ice high above the clouds where nothing should exist. Nobody noticed the lurches except Agnew, who seemed intent on ignoring his surroundings.

"Where's he going now?" Preston asked delightedly. Nanda Kot, a compact peak, moved majestically round to our left, first level with us, then dropping below and behind us. We kept climbing and turning, keeping it always on our left. Suddenly the whole gigantic triangle of Nanda Devi was on our right, a vast white ridge with ice-cliffs dropping sheer for a thousand feet, and a crowning peak at the far end. I stared at it unbelievingly as it moved past, afraid that our wingtip might brush it at any moment.

Preston read my thoughts and chuckled. "Don't worry. It's at least five miles away, perhaps ten. The Himalayas are simply much too big. Remember this one is five miles high."

We flew over the saddle between the two peaks and Trisul filled the window, a cone of ice and snow. Then suddenly they were all gone, the plane staggered as the ground dropped precipitously away, and we were running south-west with the range towering behind us. Other mountains stretched away into the distance, especially a great tangle of peaks to the north-west.

"You missed some marvellous views, Agnew."

There was no reply. Agnew had been using his sick bag and was huddled in his corner.

"Poor chap. Anything we can do?"

Agnew waved the offer away. His face was green and blotchy and he didn't want company. Taylor left the cockpit and Preston thumped him on the back.

"Damned good, my boy. Very realistic. Is it likely to be any bumpier on the day? We need to be sure that everyone is in tiptop condition when the time comes."

"Could well be much rougher than this when we fly over those mountain ranges in Burma," Taylor answered, keeping a perfectly straight face and not looking at Agnew. "Some of those turbulent air pockets really leave your stomach behind. One moment it feels as if the plane is falling out of control and then you find you're getting heaved up again. Worse than the Big Dipper."

Agnew retched in sympathy.

"We can put oxygen and heaters off now. What about that picnic? Coe has had a bite already, so I'll join you, and Buisman can take his up front. Do you realise the time? I'm ravenous."

Henderson and Lewis emerged from their corners. Agnew had no appetite but I was feeling empty. There was strong coffee, a passable assortment of sandwiches and fruit cake. Now that the air had warmed up we had a rougher ride, even over the wide valley, but I found I could ignore it. Preston turned to Agnew.

"I realise you may not feel on top of the world, but in case you are in charge I wonder if there are any further tests of aircraft or personnel you'd like carried out?"

Agnew managed a feeble, "No further tests, thank you," before heaving up again.

I made a tour of inspection of the plane, glad to clutch at the girders when we lurched. It was a clever cut-price affair, and had served us well so far, but it was impossible to feel any affection for it. It was like living inside a floating sewing machine.

We had gradually lost height and were almost back at Ranchi. Coe let our speed drop further, circled the airfield and put the flaps and wheels down, easily correcting for the little side winds. "Hold tight when we touch down. We are trying a really short landing run."

A few huddled houses, a tiny market, then the perimeter fence very close below us. A feeling of suspense as our speed still fell and we crept lower – then a very firm thud and a squeal from the brakes as we landed, pulling up fast enough to pitch us all forward despite the warning. Agnew protested faintly and was sick again. I was feeling groggy myself.

The plane stopped, the engines were switched off and the hatch was lowered. The sudden cessation of noise made me acutely aware of other small sounds. We climbed awkwardly down, stretched and stood sheepishly in a group, unzipping our flying clothes. As we passed Agnew, a forlorn figure who had to be helped out of his Augean flying kit by one of the ground crew, Taylor asked the world in general, "What was that about not losing our appetite for this mission?"

Preston had to turn his involuntary guffaw into a diplomatic fit of coughing. When he recovered he called for an ambulance for Agnew, while he waited for our truck.

At the bottom of our track the Gurkha sergeant, Havildar Narbir, had quite fluent English and checked our passes in a businesslike fashion. Adur and Hira Lal gave us a warm welcome. Indians often have a sixth sense which enables them to match the moods of people they know, without needing to know any details. There were chairs in the early evening sunshine, tea and biscuits, and a message from Colombo: Wallace's mission had at least started well.

Buisman chose his way to celebrate this news. He ran on to the verandah, jumped up, grabbed a crossbeam with both hands and swung himself on top of it, all without apparent effort. He seemed to be made of rubber.

"I told you I make every day gymnastic. You can do this thing when you exercise enough." He jumped down, turned a cartwheel and vaulted over Preston's vast empty chair. "You see. Even Taylor could do it if he tried."

I was impressed but not attracted. Whenever I let my eyes rest on the nearby fields and woods the Himalayas still seemed to float above them, halfway up the sky. The effect was hypnotic, and I found myself almost dozing off.

Soon the others came out and Preston, delighted with the flight and the news, was anxious to cross more items off his list.

"I want that plane repainted first thing tomorrow. Conspicuously high-class, to avoid any risk of confusion. Neat, not gaudy. Silver for all the lower surfaces so it won't show up from below. All the rest can be red. I'd like one of you", and his gaze swivelled ominously on me, "to put on the trade mark of that Jap intercept unit you mentioned, and perhaps the Imperial HQ sign as well. That should erase any lingering doubt from the mind of our Major X."

I tried to pull myself together and concentrate. "I can produce the characters straight away, sir, in elegant calligraphy, but only a few inches high. You want them in official printed form, which will take longer. Can anyone else copy them on to the plane about a yard high? I'm no good at that."

Buisman said, "I should like to try that job. I can decorate quite good, or spray an auto. Find me some good brushes and I try my best."

"Pardon me, Colonel," put in Coe. "When do we put back the Jap roundels? That has to be a neat job. Nothing shoddy for a general."

"Lewis, you'd better get our airfield friends to do that tonight. Taylor, why aren't we getting the results from that daily reconnaissance of Mingaladon airfield?"

"My fault, sir. The control tower gave me both sets that are in so far."

There were some two dozen overlapping sheets in each set. He and Coe worked on the floor, angling and cutting to build up a continuous picture. Taylor presided on hands and knees, his face flushed beetroot with the effort.

"Look here," said Preston, "I told you to get yourself fitter. You'll have to lose some of that spare tyre or the plane won't leave the ground. Take more exercise – hard exercise, and stop overeating. That's an order. When you get back you can do what you like."

Taylor nodded sheepishly and started, "We run in from the south here. That takes us across one end of the main runway. Then we do a slow circuit, having a careful look at everything on the ground, as Henderson said, especially the bit outside the perimeter fence, just in case they've rumbled us and set up an ambush. That reminds me, we'll need binoculars."

"Captured Jap ones are on their way here. Go on."

"When we arrive we'll see what direction the wind is, from the windsock, and Coe may have to have some chat with ground control. As soon as we've landed we taxi back to the other end and turn round, ready for take-off. We'll keep the engines ticking over. Sometimes a hot engine can be the devil to restart, and these are new to us anyway. And so we dare not refuel, which means stopping engines for safety, so we must work out our fuel needs tonight."

"Now, what are they up to? The first set shows a plane halfway down that runway, slightly blurred as it's landing."

"I guess it's taking off," said Coe quietly.

"Never. Look at the shape of the shadow. Are you crazy?"

"Pardon me," persisted Coe. "You want to borrow my glasses? Have you noticed the angle of the flaps?"

"Pack it in you two," Preston said crisply. "It makes no difference to us. The only queer thing is that it's the only plane there. What's on the other set?"

They set these out at the other end of the room. Hira Lal looked in, saw seven people on hands and knees, gazed at us in surprise, and went out again.

Coe commented, "It's the same here. There's a plane taxiing round the perimeter, and the windsock shows he's making for the take-off end, but again there's no other plane nearby. That's mighty peculiar on a main airfield. What's going on in this corner?"

They peered more closely. "Both sets show the same. Three planes are stuck in the corner, probably undergoing maintenance, and one looks as if it's being rebuilt after a crash. So far, so good. I agree that the place doesn't look as busy as it ought to. That's a puzzle. Perhaps tomorrow's set will help."

Coe looked at Preston. "There's another question you may not want to answer yet, sir. Who is going to be deputy chief on the day, especially if the big chief is being airsick? Taylor and I can make the flying decisions, but that keeps our hands full. Buisman is up there in his turret. To jump the gun, I propose that Henderson should run the outfit. There's another reason. He's acting the General, so when we're on the ground at Mingaladon he can tell me something in Japanese in front of that Major without batting an eyelid, and I can act on it right away."

"I was thinking along the same lines. Henderson to deputise for whoever is in charge? Is that acceptable to you all?"

It was the obvious choice.

"While we are on that interesting subject you may like to know that I have just sent a signal to our General in answer to his. It reads: 'REGRET AGNEW AIRSICK THROUGHOUT TRIAL FLIGHT STOP NOW IN HOSPITAL STOP NO COMMENT STOP PRESTON'. Remember the Japanese proverb: 'There is no pleasure like watching an old and valued friend fall from his roof.'

I tried to catch his ironical eye, but failed.

"An earlier dinner tonight, I think, and we'll talk shop later. I am going to celebrate today's events by wallowing in a bath."

He sang jauntily while he had it; one of the Verdi baritone arias, I think, and this time he left the text as the librettist intended.

Meanwhile Buisman and I had time to plan the painting details. I scrounged some kitchen paper from Adur and drew the characters in my boldest hand. I was feeling really tired and dizzy, and found it hard to get the swelling and tapering curves right. They seemed to swim and my hands were shaky.

Buisman whistled. "How precise must it be?"

"Exactly right or they'll know it's a fake at one glance. It's an art form for them. But these flourishes and sweeps must look spontaneous too – you know what I mean?"

"Ja, ja, I know it. We say spontaan. But I think I don't can't do it."

Then I remembered the modern style, with squared-off characters, chunky rectangular lines and hardly any hooks and sweeps. I had seen aircraft photographed with those markings, and they would be far easier for us to copy. I painted them as large as the paper allowed, each about three feet square. Then I went outside to get fresh air.

Lewis was leaning on the verandah rail. I asked him what he honestly thought about the whole scheme. He avoided giving a direct answer.

"If anyone can make it work, the Colonel's the man. He keeps a loose rein, and he's flexible about details, unlike most brass hats. But deep down he has a perfectly clear idea of all the essentials. I'd wager my savings on it." He looked at me earnestly. "I wouldn't have stayed with him if I hadn't trusted him more than I trust myself. It's true what he said: he's recommended me for a commission, more than once. I've always turned it down. Why? Because I've no idea where I might be sent. I'd rather be a sergeant with him than an officer somewhere else. He's the most sensible and objective person I know. That's why he's got this spectacular record of successes – which is why they gave him this job."

"But are you staying in the Army when the war's over?"

"Not on your life. I'm a Welsh schoolteacher, and that's what I'm itching to get back to. No peace-time soldiering for me, Preston or not."

He flipped his cigarette in a glowing arc.

"Besides, I've got a wife and a young son at home. I wouldn't want them caught up in Service life. I bet you he will be out as fast as I am."

"Won't you find it boring after all this excitement?"

"I've had enough of that to last me all my life. Another time I'd be a pacifist – that's the way my instinct runs. I didn't quite have the courage to say so in 1939."

Conversation over dinner centred on mountains. Preston had done a lot of climbing of the simpler sort, he said. No ropes, no ice-axes, just high hill-walking by himself or with a few friends, cooking and carrying for themselves. Often they would be invited into local houses or tents for the night.

"The way these people, who have practically nothing, are happy to share it with complete strangers like us, who have so much, never ceases to astonish me. It's the Islamic tradition of hospitality. The further you get off the beaten track, the more generous and pressing they are. Of course you may get unspeakable things to eat and bugs in your sleeping bag. But if that worries you, you're wasting your time anyway."

Buisman lit a small cheroot and countered with an account of climbing one of the Javanese volcanoes that was dormant rather than extinct, "... like the Dutch administration in the East Indies. They are good men and they work hard but they are sitting on the safety valve and they don't know that. They don't train no Indonesians for no jobs. I think here you do it better."

Taylor stared at him. "What do you mean, training natives for jobs? They are all right for fanning and fishing, that sort of thing, but even then the wogs never do a decent day's work. Administration? Don't make me laugh. They can't plan ahead. They've only just come down from the trees. Look at the mess Indians make of any arrangement – always late, always excuses ..."

"Excuse me," Buisman put in very calmly. "Do you say that natives are no good at work, so that white men must always run their countries as colonies?"

Taylor pulled a face. "Generally speaking, yes, I do,"

"Then let me tell you I am half a native. My mother died when I was so small. She was Javanese. My father was Dutch." His voice rose. "So am I what you call a wog, or only a half-wog? Is Coe a wog? Is he black or white or yellow? You are not white at all, you are red-face. Do you want me out of this team or only half out?" He leaned threateningly towards Taylor. "Which half will you prefer? Do I call you Tuan White Man or Mr British native? You are always blaming other people when you forget …"

Preston intervened. "That's enough of that. There will be no more talk about race and colour from either of you. This team will stay exactly as it is. Anyone who wants to withdraw for any good reason will come and tell me so privately. Anyone who threatens to break the team up will be thrown out. Is that quite clear to everyone here?"

"Aren't we entitled to personal opinions?" Taylor asked truculently.

"You are as long as you aren't personally offensive. If you haven't the sense to steer clear of trouble with the rest of the team, you'll be returned to unit at once."

Taylor said nothing.

"Don't you believe me? Coe and Buisman will take over as pilots. You'd better decide this minute."

He stared straight at Taylor until he mumbled a sort of apology. Coe looked as if he wanted to say something, but thought better of it. Buisman went on, a shade rashly. "But let me say a good word to compliment the Dutch. I think they make better roads and bridges than the British. Everything here looks like it is falling down and washing away. Even the Britishers' houses here, they are so second-rate. No beauty, just chi-chi little boxes. I stay in one just one night. That bedroom wallpaper, you know what it was? Blue roses and grey leaves and chocolate background. Must they be blind or crazy? Excuse me, Colonel."

"Gentlemen, there's business to be done, mostly about the flight We made the range 900 miles out, 600 back, 1500 in all. What mileage do you get out of this crate?"

Coe said, "That airplane will do over 2,000 miles at 150 m.p.h., but we need to cruise at 250 and go up to 330 in an emergency, so that could use it up at nearly twice the rate. I reckon we have to fit another real big tank, say 400 gallons, for a proper reserve." Taylor and Buisman nodded.

"Right. Lewis, yet another night-shift job for your friends. If that tank isn't in stock tell them to pinch it from another plane. Next point: you are flying the operation from Cox's Bazaar but where are you starting from? It's too far from here if you are all to be fresh for the whole trip. I'm afraid that means spending the previous night at Agartala, much as I loathe the dump, so how does the timing work out? Leave Agartala 0800, arrive Cox's Bazaar 0900. Allow an hour there to refuel and check, leaving at 1000. Arrive Rangoon-Mingaladon 1330. Are my sums right?"

The pilots jotted down figures, exchanged comments and agreed.

"It's close enough," said Henderson. "We said 1315 in our signal, but it's important that we shouldn't be hanging around. I don't want to wait for a mere Major. Let him wait for a General. That's his privilege."

"You've started pulling rank early, but I'll allow it this once. Next, personal preparations. You've got your flying kit so get the right badges of rank fastened on. I'm supplying the documentation. All your personal possessions are to be left here under lock and key – and I emphasise *all*. Papers, diaries, identity cards, watches, wedding rings, the lot. That must be checked and double-checked. Jap watches will be issued to you all; so will your personal survival kits. The plane will also carry two Jap inflatable life rafts, which are just being tested.

"If you have to jump or make a forced landing after getting the book, two of you are to take it and make for the nearest friendly tribal area and make contact with us through the local Force 136 people, while the rest go off in a different direction to draw off the pursuit. That's the official line. In practice you must hold a brief council of war and Henderson will make the final decision. There are always too many unknown factors for us to predict the best thing to do."

I shivered violently, and he gave me a questioning look, but went on.

"That leaves disguise. Tomorrow you will all go to Doranda military hospital, the other side of Ranchi, where you will meet Mr Sen Gupta, one of the two hundred Sen Guptas of Doranda, and his valued assistant Mr Srivastava. They are masters of their craft, which is dyes. They will dye your hair a glossy jet black and the rest a dingy yellowy-khakie with personal variations. It should last a month. Then you'll be photographed for your identity cards, which are on their way. The dye-wallahs have been told that you need to pass as Chinese, but they may guess. Don't worry; we do a lot of business with them."

All this was in the classic Secret Service tradition, but it felt wrong. Why? None of us jibed at using a Jap bomber with Jap markings to steal a Jap codebook by using a bogus signal, so it could hardly have been a moral objection.

I suddenly knew two things. The first was abject terror. Why should it happen now, when we had known the dangers all along? It seemed to be focused not on the risk that the operation might go wrong, but on being unequal to it anyway. This was not fear of death – or, far worse, of falling into Japanese hands alive – but fear of being afraid.

The second was overdue: my shivery and feverish symptoms had nothing to do with the weather – they meant a return bout of malaria. Fortunately I had plenty of mepacrine and could take the maximum dose. I was determined that nobody was going to haul me out and put me in hospital. Almost as appalling as my sudden panic was the prospect of cooing sympathy if I withdrew and something went badly wrong: "You *were* lucky to be left behind." Luck can be a terrible stigma. I was only half aware that these two ideas pointed in opposite directions.

Meanwhile Henderson was dealing energetically with a practical issue. "Colonel, may we go back to the question of disguise? I can't see the logic of it. Perhaps someone pale-skinned or fair-haired like me would benefit from shoe polish or suntan lotion. But this head-to-toe scheme is nonsense. If we have to bail out it's no use going to friendly natives for help, because we'll be Jap-coloured all over. We can't show them where the dye stops because it doesn't, and it won't wash off. And we shan't have any papers to show who we are. They will know us for Japs and the more pro-British they are, the worse it'll be for us. It's crazy."

Preston nodded fervently. "We raised precisely those objections from the start. I'm sorry to say it's an order from Colombo. As Mountbatten's in the USA we can't get him to overrule it. Apparently it's based on lessons learnt when some operation went wrong. I tried to change it two days ago. You may have heard me setting the line on fire?

"At a pinch, if the whole team refused to comply, as you've every right to do, we'd report that to Ceylon. Frankly I'm afraid they wouldn't budge. All that would happen is delay or cancellation. That's my guess. I'm not trying to cajole you, you understand. I'm sure you're right."

Henderson looked round the group. None of us thought that we could succeed where Preston and the General had failed. Delay was the last thing we wanted.

"I'd be very willing to pass on a message to Ceylon that the team unanimously agrees to this only under protest, and that the General and I associate ourselves with that protest."

"As a matter of principle, sir, I think we should welcome that."

"Then you may leave that with me, gentlemen. Now I have another contribution. Henderson, you will kindly stand. I, Anthony Erasmus Preston, temporarily Emperor of Japan, Ruler of the Nine Oceans, Holder of the Sacred Chrysanthemum, Hereditary Keeper of the Flying Dragon, do appoint thee, Donald Glenaffric Ben Nevis Henderson, presently Major in the hated, corrupt and perfidious British Army, to be our Trusty and Well-Beloved Major-General Yamaji, and thereunto", reaching across the table, "I endow thee with the Order of the Holy Pineapple, to have and to hold," placing it in the astonished Henderson's hands.

"Alan Martyn, currently Lieutenant in the aforesaid decadent and sabre-rattling British Army, you are hereby elevated to be our Honourable Colonel Miyaguchi, and admitted to the Distinguished Order of this Celestial Coffee-Pot. Neither of you, alas, draws any extra pay, even in yen. And woe betide Henderson if he tries to pull rank on *me* during his brief generalship.

"I'm going to turn in. Thank you for that trip to some of my favourite haunts. Goodnight."

Wallace Tells His Story: II

The next morning Lee and I woke, refreshed but stiff, to hear rain pattering down, though the treetops carried such a thick canopy of ferns that little reached us. We had a quick breakfast and then Lee looked at my wrist. After some probing he decided that nothing was broken but there was a bad sprain.

"Try a little traditional Chinese magic. My mother taught me this when I was a boy."

His flexible fingertips pushed more deeply into the recesses, very patiently, and he took my right palm as if we were shaking hands and pulled steadily on it while he kneaded the wrist with his other hand. Suddenly there was a click and at once the pain lessened. He massaged it for some time and then brought out of an inside pocket one of those tiny red tins of 'Tiger Balm' that made Aw Boon Haw a Singapore millionaire. I knew it well. It's a pungent embrocation and counter-irritant and works wonders on ailments like this. The advertisements claimed success against everything short of death itself. He rubbed some into the wrist and gave me the tin. By now my elbow felt less painful but was still very stiff, and he made up a sling that helped.

There was no doubt about our next priority – to get the bogus signal off to Rangoon. It had to go as soon as their regular mid-day schedule finished, normally about 1230–1245, but before that we had to find a safer place to set up the aerial and go ahead the moment the enemy schedule ended. Could we manage it?

We unpacked the first radio and found it had suffered in the drop. Lee fiddled with the innards but it stayed obstinately dead.

We tried the other and it was all right. We covered up the rest of our cache with ferns and creepers, picked up the good radio and our tommy-guns, and started towards the north-west, aiming for a smaller peak north of the main summit.

The difficulty was to keep moving in the right direction. The textbooks say: 'Take a bearing on the course you want to follow, and notice what object stands on that line. Then march towards it.' Unfortunately each tree changed character as we wove our way among the great trunks, and we wasted time arguing which was which. In the end we trusted to instinct.

At last we came out on the edge of the trees and looked northwards through our binoculars. In the distance was Gunung Tiong, a hazy grey-green mass with low clouds shrouding the peak. The valley along which we had flown last night ran across quite close below us, with two straggling villages clearly visible. Nearer still men and women were working in the paddy fields despite the rain, and to our right was a rubber plantation with estate buildings which we must have been uncomfortably close to when we dropped. There was no sign of any Japanese, but their everyday uniforms were so drab and nondescript that we couldn't be sure.

One look at the peak we had wondered about ruled it out. Reaching it would mean crossing open ground where we might be spotted and could easily be cut off and surrounded. Instead we found a more promising area further up the hill we were on. But again this brought problems. The high trees that had sheltered us stopped and were replaced by thorn bushes and bamboo growing in slippery mud. It became difficult to stop ourselves slithering backwards, and when we clutched at the bushes for support they tore our hands. With my right arm temporarily useless I was even worse placed than Lee. A fine pair of agents, I thought.

Just then we heard an aircraft over to the west, near where the Australians had dropped their bombs last night. At any moment it might fly our way, so we tried to retrace our steps. Going downhill is always more tricky than climbing up, and it was vital not to twist an ankle. Then the plane came into view, a small twin-engined

machine that buzzed round and round, very low. We were in our
long camouflage jackets and knew that if we kept stock-still we
would be all right, but the lower it came the harder it was not to
follow our instinct and run. In the end it suddenly turned and flew
off. We hoped he hadn't seen us and gone back to report.

It was now mid-morning and at this rate we would not get the
signal off today. Damn Preston and his banter and his hare-brained
scheme. Damn Martyn and his extra-long, extra-special, clever-
clever signal. Our only course was to cut our losses, move back to
the shelter of the woods we had so foolishly left, and transmit from
there after all. We moved awkwardly back and by 1120 were under
cover again. Was it safe to leave the rest of our equipment down
below? Safe or not, we should have to chance it. Time was beginning to move against us. We hoped the Japs were not.

We soon found a hollow where we should be out of sight at least
from casual passers-by, and set up the aerial. Although my wrist was
easier now, I knew that Lee must send the signal, as absolute fluency was essential. He unpacked the radio, put on his earphones
and tuned to the Singapore–Rangoon frequency. There were our
familiar operators in their midday schedule, closer and clearer with
Singapore only fifty miles behind us. Lee got out the signal text
from Ranchi and we filled in the blank space with the cipher group
that gave the day after tomorrow as the date for the codes to be
picked up – the earliest day they could guarantee to be ready. We
checked over the procedure and preamble that had been agreed.
We were ready to break in.

While I kept a lookout, Lee listened intently and told me what
was happening. "Another message just started." He disconnected
his key and coolly began practising his Japanese Morse for extra
fluency while he listened in. "Hold on, message ends. No, here's
another one." This could go on for quite a time, so I unpacked the
rest of our first day's rations and shared them between us. Outside
the wood the rain was pelting down, but little of it reached us, and
although we were bitterly cold our clothes were beginning to dry
out.

1215. "This is a very long message, Sam." Only my absolute confidence in Lee kept my frustration at a bearable level. Here I was, having trained for months for this vital job – by which I meant my guerrilla work, not this daft signal – and all I could do was injure myself the moment I landed. But remorse was no use. I wasn't ambidextrous. Trying to use a Morse key at all, with a stiff arm and a shaky wrist, would have been stupid. Using it for this signal, with the need to mimic Japanese style perfectly, would be foolhardy and could destroy the whole operation. Lee was at least as good an operator as I was, I reminded myself sternly.

"Message ends. Another message." The time crept on from 1230 to 1245. "Message ends. Ah! They're signing off. Wish me luck, Sam." He took a deep breath.

This was our big moment, and I literally crossed my fingers for him. There seemed to be a lot of chitchat with the Rangoon operator, and he was using the usual jargon, which was not in code and I could understand. He seemed calmer than ever.

Here it was. His key began to rattle with a beautifully convincing touch that I could savour as if I were using it myself. I imagined the flutter in the Rangoon dovecotes when the reference to Imperial HQ hit them. A little pause, then the familiar opening groups of the bogus signal itself, which I had practised so hard. There was nothing I could do to help, except to keep an eye open for intruders.

At last it was finished and he signed off. "No problems at all. He took it like a lamb. Shall I confirm to Colombo right away?"

Ranchi needed as much notice as possible, so he changed the frequency and called up our HQ. Force 136 used the international ham procedures, so there was nothing to betray our call apart from the agreed five-digit group meaning 'PAPERCHASE SIGNAL SENT'. We had arranged that for the first forty-eight hours they would listen round the clock for our signals, and there was no pause before they replied and Lee sent the signal in his usual fist. I was impressed by the imperturbable way in which he changed his personality between Allied Jekyll and Japanese Hyde.

Now we had to wait several hours before the signals Major at Rangoon confirmed that he had received our message and would comply with it. We talked over our own immediate plans. The loads were safely cached for the time being and it seemed wise to leave them there and stay in this wood tonight. After that we had plenty to get on with. Tomorrow Lee would go down to the valley road further west in civilian clothes and discreetly sound out some of the labourers. If they thought it was safe he would make his way to Kluang, ten miles away, and try to contact the most promising of his pre-war friends, assuming the Japanese had not picked him up for the guerrilla activities which Lee felt sure he was engaged in. Once he had met him he would return, he hoped with some helpers.

We felt elated but worn out. The sudden transition from the relatively sophisticated surroundings and routines of Colombo to the rustic tradition of eastern Malaya, and the thought of the unknown hazards of the next twenty-four hours, let alone one or two years, had a hypnotic effect. I only now realised that we *were* back in Malaya. I could almost smell the savoury market smells: stalls selling lumpur, those handily shaped snacks of rice and chicken-meat rolled up in a banana leaf, and the clove-scented cigarettes. The breath-taking excitement had passed. The long hard slog was about to begin.

Meanwhile we brewed some rice and added to it one of Lee's favourites, tinned sardines. Dried apricots and coffee followed. We took it in turns to rest while the other kept watch, and Lee was dozing when I heard twigs cracking some way off. I roused him and we listened. There were voices. Whoever they belonged to, they were making no effort to move quietly. That could mean Chinese or Japanese, but not the Malays, who were unlikely to be up in the woods, nor the local Sakai tribesmen, who moved too softly to be heard. They seemed to be moving in a line that would bring them close to us. We cocked our guns and freed the safety catches.

Suddenly Lee whispered, "They're speaking Hakka. I'll go and see who they are." He got up and walked towards them, calling out Hakka greetings as he went; these guerrillas were often terribly trigger-happy. There was a tense silence, then a roar of laughter.

He returned with three cheerful, boisterous and ruffianly Chinese. They all carried guns as if they knew how to use them. Naturally they had forgotten the password – hence the hilarity.

"We had a message about you, and then we heard a plane last night. A friend in the first village over there, Kampong Kahang, said there had been parachutists over this side of the road, so we guessed you might be up here. He thought at least ten men had been dropped. Those big explosions damaged the railway station and woke me up at my home in Kampong Gajah, the next village up the road. I am Lau Sang and these are my comrades, Ah Bing and Whu Lim."

We shook hands self-consciously, and squatted or sat while we found out more about each other.

"We are part of the Communist Chinese group which controls the resistance between Kluang and the east coast."

This sounded rather grandiose, and we found later that like most such statements it was exaggerated, but at least they would have local support, which was what we needed. We introduced ourselves as Allied officers but said no more.

"Our area leader for the patriotic struggle is Tan Chuen and I am his deputy. We are on good terms with the Sakai, and their chief Panjang is very helpful. They will carry your loads. Have you brought any arms for our men?"

Lee explained that we had an urgent signal to receive in a few hours' time, and everything else must wait till that was complete. In country areas the Chinese or Malay concept of time is inexact, and they could not see why it mattered to receive a signal at a fixed time. How did we know that it would come? If we told them where our stores were, they could have them moved at once. It took all Lee's patient diplomacy to insist that the signal came first, and that we would not show them our cache till then. Both of us knew that some guerrillas were interested only in the weapons that we brought in, which they would sell for profit or use to extort ransom money from rich or nervous Chinese businessmen. These three men seemed plausible enough, but it would be foolhardy to trust them whole-heartedly too soon.

I decided to probe further. I asked Lau if he knew Chu Mei. This was a trap. Chu Mei was a notorious informer who had already betrayed several Chinese and British agents, and as the Chinese often speak highly of people that they think the other person likes, he might speak warmly of Chu. To my relief Lau denounced him without hesitation, and said he had got himself a safe job in Kuala Lumpur out of their reach, otherwise he would have been killed long before. All this I knew. So far, so good. What about Ah Ching and Chin Peng? He had heard their names and believed they were good men; that was all he could tell us. I tried Lim Han, a fictitious name: no reaction.

"Do you know anyone from Pahang, where I used to work?"

He pondered. "I have met Lah Leo at a planning meeting and heard many good things about him since."

That clinched it. Some of the local guerrilla leaders had more blarney and bravado than commonsense, but Lah Leo was a modest man, one of the best leaders in my old area, who never promised anything he could not accomplish.

So Lee and I agreed that as soon as our signal was dealt with, we would join forces with them, though I should be staying south of the valley road while he moved further north.

They wanted to see how Lee sent a signal, so after unobtrusively disconnecting the key from the set he sent out a Morse signal, and then lent them the headphones in turn to hear the Singapore-Rangoon signals traffic. We thought it might puzzle or dismay them if they knew it was not an Allied but an enemy link. They were as pleased as schoolboys.

We weren't sure when our reply might come, so we fixed 2000 hrs, an hour after the last specified time, for our rendezvous at the foot of the hill. We told them to bring eight Sakai, no more and no less, to carry our loads, and to make absolutely sure that they weren't followed. They promised faithfully to do as we said, and trudged off in high spirits.

The first possible time for the acknowledgment, 1700, came and went uneventfully. We could picture Major X wrestling with his decoding and wondering what on earth to do about the message. We played cards for an hour. In the tropics sunset varies very little and arrives very suddenly, so we were relieved when at the second appointment, 1800, we heard Rangoon loud and clear, confirming that our message had been received and understood by transmitting the specified groups 1234 1234 rather laboriously, as befitted a Major out of practice. As soon as he paused we acknowledged with a slick 6789 6789, and the transaction was complete. Wonderful! Lee sent off our second message to Colombo, signifying 'PAPERCHASE ACCEPTED', and the plan was firmly booked.

Feeling really pleased with ourselves we packed up and made our way through the trees. Our cache was undisturbed. Act One of the operation had gone almost without a hitch, and now the Ranchi team would be getting ready for their extraordinary code-snatch attempt.

That still haunted me. I saw the logic of the scheme and appreciated the ingenuity of the details, but one stroke of bad luck in the weather or the flight, or some trivial misunderstanding at Rangoon or delay on the return run – any discrepancy – could turn it into a tragedy. I was puzzled that the team members, who seemed bright enough to work that out for themselves, were still willing to put their heads in the noose, as if they were betting on a certainty. Well, we had completed our bit of the plot, and perhaps we should learn one day how the rest had gone. Meanwhile it was time to rendezvous with our new friends.

INTERLUDE: HASHIMOTO HAS HIS LUNCH

Major Hashimoto was enjoying his lunch. It had taken some time to find a restaurant in Rangoon which offered not only decent food but also surroundings which were clean, tasteful, comfortable and not too obviously Burmese. The 'New Asian Pagoda', though not sumptuous, formed a harmonious whole. Harmony, a proper balance, appealed to him. It was presumably his balance of tact, expertise and dependability that had secured him his promotion to Major and his new job as Commanding Officer of the Signals Unit of the Fifth Air Division at Rangoon, when old Saito had been posted to a less demanding job at Singapore.

Two years at Prome had been more than enough. The town – or city as it liked to call itself – was little more than a railhead and river-port. Men and stores came up by rail, and casualties went back. Some rice still went down the river, and supplies were supposed to come up it too. But during the last year enemy aircraft had been strafing the trains and boats every day, almost unopposed, and the constant danger had altogether banished the antique charm of the great pagoda and the picturesque but shabby little houses and overgrown gardens of the former British civil servants.

It was a long time since he had last squatted on the straw-mat floor of a Japanese restaurant, and he was still getting used to Burmese ideas of food. This was some sort of fish soup, but where was the succulent seaweed that should accompany it? When had he last tasted *tataki*, that fragrant dish of tuna fillet, lightly toasted over glowing pine needles and served with garlic and soya sauce? And when you made the proper noises of appreciation any non-Japanese there turned and stared, or even laughed. Fortunately there were not many. The 'New Asian Pagoda' was becoming more selective.

He was still reconciling himself to the slipshod way in which things happened in Burma: the groups of blank-faced monks, of every age from the cradle to the grave, wearing saffron robes and shuffling along with their begging bowls. The palmists foretelling improbable futures, the water-carriers straining off some very dubious drinking water, the old women with wrinkled faces selling, and even smoking, those ferocious green cheroots.

Now for the raw fish. There was no real tang in the taste; this seemed to be the best the manager could produce.

Then there was the question of religion. His father had been a Shinto disciple, and he himself had imperceptibly inherited something of the doctrine of natural virtue. The whole family had visited the shrine of the Sun-Goddess Amaterasu at Ise while he was still a schoolboy, and despite the pressing crowds of pilgrims he had sensed the divine awe that it was steeped in. In Japan those beliefs were largely absorbed into Buddhism, and here he was, in one of its main centres. All around him spirits were being appeased and good works performed to acquire merit.

He had done his share. He had been more than a mere tourist visiting the pagodas. He had bought his obligatory bits of gold leaf to stick on them, although it was obvious that the next shower would wash them off. From time to time he recited the Japanese Buddhist prayer of the Lotus Sutra. More importantly he had felt those inklings urging renunciation of the vain illusions of life.

But again this meant a balancing trick – in fact a tightrope act. How could you believe that all ideas were illusions and yet be a loyal and patriotic officer in the Imperial Army? Wartime propaganda was now fervently linking Goddess-worship with Emperor-worship. But how could you reconcile the more brutal aspects of Bushido with the compassion demanded by Buddha? It was all very difficult.

Here at last was the shellfish course with plenty of rice. The small boy who brought it knew his preferences now, and had reminded the cook to make it as like tempura as possible, with a spicy mixture of prawn and lobster served really hot. He smiled approvingly and looked around the room as he ate. He noticed the garish rows of sugary fruit drinks which probably contained a high proportion of water from the Rangoon creeks, the tinted photographs of pagodas and – more approvingly – the bowls and plates in front of him. They had been brought in from Japan, and reminded him of his favourite fish restaurant at home. The shapes were elegant and the painted decoration perfect.

"More tempura, boy. Make sure it's hot again. Hotter still. And bring some saké."

It arrived quickly and he continued eating. There were other officers there whom he knew by sight, and he was senior to most of them. Two Colonels from Burma Area Army HQ were in a far corner. They often sat there and he felt puzzled at their being so secluded, almost secretive. Higher-ranking officers generally ate in the main HQ mess, where he didn't yet feel at home. Most of them were from Tokyo. He was from Osaka, that cheerful city where the greeting is, "How much money are you making?" That was no reason for treating him like a country bumpkin.

That was another thing. You had to hold the balance between being so militaristic that you turned coarse and brutish, and so peace-loving that you became a mere student of military affairs, an academic in uniform. He knew examples of each. There was that terrible barbarian Colonel Tsuji at one extreme, the fire-eater, and bespectacled Colonel Yoshikawa at the other, a reclusive medico, almost a monk. Neither reflected much credit on the Emperor. There must be a golden mean – a European phrase admittedly, but corresponding to a proper Oriental concept.

Finally there was this morning's letter from his wife, Yasuko, who seemed to be facing the same sort of choice. She was a secondary school teacher, and much of her slender spare time, when preparations were done, went on the innumerable patriotic committees raising money for various war purposes: charities for the disabled and the widows, or buying a plane to defend the homeland. But their two children also needed more time spent on them. Their daughter, Emiko, was at secondary school and making good steady progress. Shinji was a year older and would soon be in the Army himself. The boy seemed to understand the implications of this without fully accepting them. Yet when he himself had some home leave and tried to open the subject tactfully, he found he could make no headway.

Perhaps it was not surprising. The war had been going badly in the Pacific for over a year, and now even the British, whom they had kicked out of Burma with their tails between their legs, seemed to be rising from the grave and pushing them back after defeating them in the north. Worse still, there were rumours of quarrels between senior officers, who were being replaced, doubtless by other excellent men, rather too quickly for comfort.

As signals officer at a headquarters he had a good picture of what was happening up there, and knew that only a false impression was reaching the public in Japan. That probably meant that the situation elsewhere was graver than the press admitted. There was plenty to worry about near at hand. Far from getting the reinforcements they needed, they were losing some of the men and equipment they already had – sending them to Indo-China, as if there weren't enough shortages here already. His own unit was still awaiting some radio spares ordered six months ago, and it was only the ingenuity of his staff and, he thought he could add, his capable direction that kept it in full operational readiness. The Burmese, too, were not so docile as they had been at first. It was no longer safe to post a sentry in an isolated position at night. He was dead next morning.

But it was no use letting these things prey on your mind; he must relax while he had an hour away from the job.

"Boy, bring me some mangoes if they are fresh."

Now that *was* a useful Burmese contribution to a meal, but you had to check every one, or goodness only knew what disease you might catch. The first, at least, tasted just as it should. He had never come across better ones than those beauties in Singapore, the first time he had tasted them. Durian, on the other hand, which some people claimed had the most delicate flavour of all, unfortunately smelt like drains, or worse. He preferred not to think about them at mealtime.

The door opened and Lieutenant Kakimura entered, his second-in-command, a promising and zealous young officer, but too easily flustered. He came across to the table, saluted and bent forward.

"Excuse me, please, Major, for interrupting your lunch. There is an urgent signal for you."

Hashimoto sighed. "Sit down, Kakimura. What is it about, this signal?"

"I cannot tell, sir." He lowered his voice and leaned across the table. "The cipher clerk decoded only the preamble, which said it was for your eyes only, from Imperial HQ, a special message."

Hashimoto stared at him. "You have seen this signal yourself?"

"Only those first few groups, sir. I checked his work carefully myself before coming here and disturbing you at your meal. The signal is now locked in the safe. I have left Sergeant Kadota in charge."

"Very well. I must certainly come myself."

He pushed the food away, settled the bill, saluted the Colonels and made his way to the car Kakimura had brought. Democratic tendencies urged him to sit in front; tradition suggested the back. He chose the back.

It was quite extraordinary to have to wrestle with a codebook again. In his days as a cipher clerk, before he had been commissioned, that had been a regular task, and he flattered himself that he had been second to none of his colleagues in speed and accuracy. Now it was an irksome chore. He couldn't trust his memory; even the commonest groups had to be looked up. Fortunately all the preliminary deciphering had been done, and he had only the last stage, the actual decoding, to do himself. As he worked through what was obviously a long message he found it difficult to grasp at first reading.

Everything about it was highly unusual.

Messages did not come straight from Imperial HQ as a rule, but via Southern Army at Manila. They were packing up to move back to Saigon; was that perhaps the explanation? As for the Tokushu Joho Bu – that was something never talked about. It was said to be intercepting and reading enemy signals; anything you heard about it you had to forget instantly. As with any hush-hush unit, rumours abounded, and the combination with Imperial HQ was awe-inspiring. Something must have gone terribly wrong: some deplorable lapse in security. No wonder they were avoiding the usual channels. He had already banished his staff; now he locked the door.

The *new* book compromised! He drew in his breath noisily. Risking the old one would have been bad enough, but to lose the new one would be a disaster. Could this be the work of those damned long-range penetration groups, the Chindits, as the British idiotically called them, who were coming in by glider in large groups, severing road and rail links and threatening troops who had thought themselves well away from trouble? Apparently they had not merely brought in anti-aircraft defences but had impertinently cleared an airstrip and were operating Spitfires from it. Perhaps they had been lucky enough to pick up a copy of the new codebook if they had overrun a signals unit. If so, why hadn't he been told? But of course there was no proof that it had happened in Burma. The book was used over a huge area of the Pacific. Probably the island-hopping Yankees had been lucky, as usual.

Now there was all this rigmarole about taking his copy to the airfield. No special problem there, and if he couldn't invent a plausible reason for being there, he would be very much surprised. As for the paraphernalia of passwords, signal destruction certificate, personal acknowledgement, and possibly a hint in the last paragraph of a medal, or at least a commendation – that was quite extraordinary. But then the whole affair must be of extreme importance for a General to be collecting the book himself. Certainly the arrangements were admirably designed to maintain complete secrecy.

There was much to be done before sending his reply at the first opportunity. He must act circumspectly. If anything went wrong with his part of the programme he would have no written authority to produce. Being a cautious man he resolved, against all the orders, to keep a private record of what the signal said, in case he needed it to justify his actions once he had obediently destroyed the signal.

It suddenly dawned on him that his hesitancy sprang from an intuitive fear that this might be an incredibly clever enemy plot. Something – he could not put his finger on it – didn't ring true. Surely he ought to consult someone in HQ, perhaps Major-General Akabane, who had overall responsibility for signals. But that would mean going against the explicit instruction: 'to be known only to yourself'. Moreover Akabane was a stickler. And though this Major-General Yamaji ranked no higher than Akabane, behind him loomed the mysterious figures of Field-Marshals and the almost divine presence of Supreme Headquarters.

Besides, how could the enemy be sending a message from Singapore at all, especially one which used the current code system and revealed so intimate a knowledge of his network, let alone flying one of the Emperor's aircraft? Yet that nagging doubt still lodged at the back of his mind and could not be stilled.

Here was a nice dilemma for him, and he had to decide quickly. He couldn't even tell which course was playing safe, where this most unusual order was concerned: obeying or disobeying it. He knew what he must do. His early Shinto upbringing had taught him that a man's conscience is his best guide. He must meditate carefully and make a choice that would bring natural virtue and enlightened patriotism into a coherent whole.

There must be no rash decision. Discipline and logic pointed clearly in one direction: obeying the signal. But his instincts warned him that he might be making a terrible mistake. With the way the war was going now, shouldn't he trust his instincts?

He composed himself for thought.

Day Six:
The General Comes To Dinner

At Ranchi we woke early with rain drumming on the corrugated-iron roof. From there it cascaded down and turned the verandah into a swimming pool, overflowed to join a torrent from further up the hill, and swelled a muddy river which ran down beside the track and swirled into a brown pool where it joined the road. Two Gurkhas in capes ran up the lane and sheltered on the cookhouse verandah, their ear-to-ear smiles unimpaired. I was glad that Preston claimed to have some authority over them. They were renowned as fighters, but showed scant respect for anyone other than their own Gurkha officers. (I knew of a surgeon Colonel running a hospital who caught two of them milking cows kept especially for the patients. He remonstrated with them. "Yougotohell," they said, standing to attention, full of smiles. An appeal to their Havildar, a mere Sergeant, stopped them at once.) We dressed more warmly than usual, pulling on sweaters that had long been packed away. My head swam as I balanced on one leg to pull on trousers.

"I've got news for you all," Preston said at breakfast. "Tonight the General is coming from Comilla to dine with us. He wants to look at you, after which I hope he will approve our team of volunteers. There will be no great ceremony, but I assume you will wish to look smarter than slum-dwellers going carol singing. We shall meet for drinks at 1900 and dine at 1930.

"Adur, who is responsible for the weather, assures me that this downpour will finish in two hours. Martyn, you look a bit down in the mouth. Are you sickening for something?"

"I think I've got a touch of malaria. I had a bad attack last year and it creeps back occasionally."

"Right, mepacrine for you in large doses, even if it makes you look like a fried egg. We've got plenty here if you run out. If it gets worse you say so at once, you hear?"

"Coe, I've had a signal asking for you to be returned without delay. You are needed to evaluate some new Jap wonder-plane that has been captured. What shall I tell them?"

Coe pulled a face. "Say it can wait, sir. Maybe 'Not known at this address'?"

"My thoughts exactly. I shall reply 'COX UNKNOWN HERE STOP TRY COX'S BAZAAR', and by the time they signal 'FOR COX READ COE', we shall have thought of some less crude dodge, if we're still here. I'll carry the can later."

"Now, the General wants to know more details of our outward flight, which he has to clear with Colombo. I take it there's no change for the first leg, Agartala to Cox's Bazaar?"

"No, sir," said Taylor. "It's a commuting trip for me, and I can't imagine any snags. For the next stretch we go right out into the Bay of Bengal, flying at our ceiling."

"That's news to me," Coe said. "I'd say it's better on the deck."

"Why?"

"Below radar cover. Less chance of being spotted over the sea. No danger of being spotted from below. Maximum surprise. It's our normal drill."

"Then forget it."

"My air college instructors said fly at nought feet to avoid detection."

"Damn your college instructors," retorted Taylor waspishly. "Use your sense. Think about our set-up. That low-flying plan is perfect for attacking the enemy, right? But we represent a friendly Jap plane flying into Jap-held Rangoon, so we don't need to worry about avoiding detection. We approach just as they would. That gives them no reason to be suspicious. There's another thing: when there's no wind the sea around here's a killer. The surface looks like glass and you can't tell how close you are. It's too close to depend on the altimeter. We lost an aircraft and crew that way last month. Just flew into the sea."

Suddenly the Oriental side of Coe won and he gave a formal smile. "You are right and I withdraw my objection. Please forgive my error."

"Anything else on the outward route?"

"I don't expect trouble till we get due south of Rangoon. Then we really have to be on our toes. There are Jap airfields due east, and we have to arrive from nowhere and become one of their planes flying due north."

Coe added, "There's another detail. When you've been sitting in flying kit several hours you can get cramp, pins and needles, that stuff. If we fly into Mingaladon like a bunch of stiffs we'll be no good."

"Maybe I take you a short race up and down the fuselage," Buisman suggested. "I don't see nobody else doing everyday gymnastic like me."

"Then that's on the agenda. Physical jerks for five at 1245 at 1,000 feet. What about the actual run-in? I spent a week there some years ago and I recall there being a hell of a lot of pagodas. None of them likely to get in your way?"

"Not unless there is very low cloud. If that happens we give the city a wide berth and come in from further north."

"Anything else about landing drill, hand-over and take-off from there?"

We groaned. We had been practising that until we could do it in our sleep.

"I sense the mood of the meeting. Now the route back?"

That was the tricky part. It depended on so many unpredictables, above all our reception at the airfield. Our provisional route was a compromise imposed on us by the need to save fuel. We had to feint towards Saigon until we were hidden in cloud, and then get back to our outward route. Coe looked worried.

"I'd be happier if we fixed the route back now as well. There's plenty to improvise without that. Why can't we fix that too: height, compass course, speed, so forth?"

"The trouble with you, Coe," Taylor snapped, "is that though you're a good pilot you're a Navy pilot. You spend your time grinding around in the middle of nowhere, from island X to island Y, with damn all between except salt water. So naturally you need a compass course. You know there's no enemy fire unless there's a ship or aircraft in sight. Overland trouble can come from anywhere without warning. We go dodging round mountains and along ravines and never know who's round the corner. We may have plenty of that on the home run.

"There's another thing. You trained as a fighter pilot, correct? You're talking as if this was a fighter mission; if it gets tough, step on the gas, jump out of the way. You can't throw a bomber around like that, especially in Burma weather. I tell you, this is not a college assignment with fancy credits and an examiner's grading. For God's sake, forget the classroom and think of the geography."

Coe was breathing hard and his eyes were furious. Preston intervened firmly but quietly. "I can't have this bickering. You've both had your say. Now I'm reminding you that while you're here I'm running this show. If you don't like it on a loose rein, I'll have to tighten it. Is that clear or do I have to knock your heads together? If you go on in this childish fashion I'll send you both back to your units and we'll start again without you."

Both of them grinned sheepishly.

"Then we'll check the details when we get the met forecast just before we leave. If there's any disagreement during the flight, Henderson will settle it. That's the end of that for now, thank God. Now until the rain stops I want you to study these maps of Burma. Learn the salient points. One of you memorise rivers, one mountains, one railways and so on. Then I'll test you on it. It's not a game. Too many ops come to grief because someone gets lost. I learnt that the hard way in 1942 over France, where I had no business to be. We were completely lost and there was continuous cloud except for one tiny gap right over a town. It lasted about ten seconds before the gap closed up. The navigator shouted, 'Turn due north, quick.' He swore it was Clermont-Ferrand because he'd seen it, in a tourist booklet, mark you, before the war. And by God, he was right. If we'd gone on any further we'd have flown slap into the mountains just south of there. So learn the salient points carefully."

I got railways. They were the easiest because there were so few. "Notice the junctions, notice the bridges," Preston said, breathing down my neck. "Now try this," plonking down a large sheet of paper covering the whole map, with a small hole in the middle. It showed a railhead beside a wide river. Obviously Prome.

"Correct, but far too easy. Try this."

It looked almost the same. I racked my brains but had to give up.

"Failed. Myingyan, near Mandalay. Taylor, what's this lake?"

He failed too. We all joined in, without result.

"Failed, the lot of you. That's Lake Indawgyi. We used it to evacuate casualties without having an airstrip. We sent in flying boats from Colombo and they flew out hundreds. They felt like fishes out of water going over those peaks east of Imphal, but the lake was just where we'd promised."

The rain stopped as predicted, the sun came out fiercely, and the whole countryside started steaming. The river shrank to a rivulet and then a muddy trench. The Gurkhas shook their caps, trudged squelchily down the track and took up position at the gate.

"Very well. A temporary reprieve. You all failed, so get to work and learn it up. Another reminder: *no* marked maps or charts are to go with you. You will take those captured Jap ones, which happen to have some Jap markings left on. Leave them as they are. I don't want even a faint pencil-line of ours to show what we're up to. That is operation-wrecker number two, in my experience.

"Now off to the airfield. I want those Jap characters painted on before lunch, and every bit of equipment thoroughly checked over. There's time for a quick coffee first. Martyn, black coffee and mepacrine for you."

At the airfield Taylor and Coe got on with their jobs on board while Buisman and I started painting the characters, helped by Henderson who could check position and proportions better from a distance.

The overnight spraying job was done and the plane reeked of paint. All the upper surfaces were crimson, and I stood on the tailplane and began painting the outlines on the big rudder. That took an hour, and then I started on the other side while Buisman filled in the outlines. The second side went much faster and the result was impressive, with the seven characters for Chuo Tokushu Joho Bu (Central Special Intelligence Department) above a row of smaller characters for Imperial HQ, all in silver. If that didn't impress Major X, nothing would. We walked round the perimeter track to clear our heads of the pungent smell that made me dizzier still, but couldn't resist looking back to admire our handiwork.

We lunched in the mess and then got down to the afternoon's tasks. Taylor, Coe and Buisman were taking the plane for a final flying check and would see how well it could be thrown about in the event of a scrap. Henderson and I were not sorry to miss that. We were trying the weapons that would be carried on the plane: Japanese machine-carbines, automatics, and tiny grenades which would deal with any opposition on the ground without damaging the aircraft.

We collected them from the armoury and drove over to the battle course, where an enthusiastic small-arms specialist initiated us into the business of loading, aiming, firing and unjamming. We leant how to keep our heads clear of the shower of empty cartridge cases, how to select single rounds or automatic, and how to find the safety catch infallibly without looking at it. Then we practised with fixed and moving targets until Preston was satisfied. We ended up by hurling some grenades to get their feel. With our eardrums singing we returned to the airfield, where the others had just landed. They had no fault to find, and the plane would now be ready for immediate use, kept in a hangar under guard.

We discussed how to deal with Major X. It would be grotesque for Henderson to interview him through the underneath hatch, where his feet would be opposite the Major's shoulders. Neither would see the other, and only a contortionist would feel at ease. There was no side door, but on each side was a 'blister', a bulbous affair holding a machine-gun, with perspex panels for visibility. Part of this could be slid open and from there Henderson could look down on the Major, who might well have to stand on tiptoe to pass him the book – a useful psychological ploy. We checked that both blisters opened fully. That was all we should need if he cooperated, but the hatch was in reserve in case stronger measures were called for.

"Right. I have banished the ground crew. I want you at action stations, as if you have just landed. I shall be Major X with his little parcel. Practise your Jap lingo and I'll do my best in my supporting role. *Action stations!*"

Taylor and Coe wormed their way through into the cockpit, Buisman clambered into his turret and then remembered and came halfway back, Henderson stood near the port blister and I was just behind him. Both of us drew our automatics, Buisman held his machine-carbine just out of sight, and there was a net of grenades at hand. Preston surveyed the scene, marched crisply up towards the plane, saw Buisman slide the blister open and Henderson appear just inside it, halted below, and threw an exaggerated musical-comedy salute.

"Good afternoon, Major," Henderson said coolly in Japanese.

"Mumbo-jumbo, sahib," replied Preston.

"You may now give me the codebook, Major."

"Here it is, General sahib," stretching upwards towards the blister with it.

"Check it, please, Colonel," said Henderson disdainfully. It was a bound volume of *Punch* for 1934.

"Quite correct, sir."

"I also require your signal destruction certificate, Major, you remember."

"Very good, sir. Here it is."

"Precisely. My receipt, Colonel, please."

I handed over an imaginary piece of paper with a flourish; Henderson passed it to Preston.

"Perfectly in order, Major. We must now leave at once. Goodbye."

Preston saluted, turned on his heels and marched away. He came back less formally.

"You can all come out now. Apart from the absence of the receipt, which we know is in hand, that seemed to run well. Any reservations? In that case we now have to postulate the Major's arriving with the book but refusing to hand it over without some further authorisation. Assuming that we cannot persuade him quickly, we have to rehearse a plausible kidnap. We therefore promote Lewis to be acting Major, Japanese Army Air Force, while I observe from within. Lewis, the codebook is yours."

Lewis, with deadpan lack of surprise, squashed his bush hat into a rough semblance of a Japanese cap. He marched up to the blister and saluted.

"Good afternoon, Major," said Henderson again.

"Blaenau ffestiniog, Llanrwst," Lewis replied with a perfectly straight face.

"You may now give me the book, Major."

"Llanfihangel-y-pennant garn dolbermaen, Llanrwst, rhiwbryfdir tanygrisiau pentre-ta-farn-y-fedw pentre-llyn-cymmer penybenglog ..."

"Never mind about that, Major. Simply hand over the book at once."

"... clwt-y-bont cwm-y-glo llanfairpwllgwyngyll efailnewydd," Lewis concluded triumphantly.

Buisman, looking dazed, was standing ready beside the hatch. Henderson motioned to him to open it and went round to the top of the steps, and I followed him. We had decided that this implicit invitation would be the most persuasive. Certainly Lewis thought so, for he now appeared below the hatch and came up a step or two.

"Come inside, Major, and let us discuss your problem in here. But hurry. We have no time to waste."

Lewis came up warily. As soon as he was inside I gave him a token bang on the head with a haversack while Buisman slammed the hatch shut.

"Take off at once," shouted Henderson in Japanese.

As we reached the truck an RAF corporal came up and saluted. "These signals have come in from Ranchi, sir, and the Sergeant sent them up for you."

Preston opened the outer envelope: one of the signals was marked for him and two for me. Mine were from Delhi. There was still no date given for bringing in the new codebook – thank God for that. The other said that they had tracked down the Rangoon air force signals Major, who had been promoted from Captain to Major and moved there from Prome two months before. Nothing else was known about him except his name, Hashimoto. Now Henderson might be able to use his name if the conversation called for it. And he was new in his post. Excellent.

Preston had slit open his envelope and was rereading the signal thoughtfully, as if unsure what to do with it. Then he took Henderson on one side, talked with him for a short while, and gave him the message. He came back to us.

"Poor Henderson's wife has been killed. Knocked down by a car in the blackout."

He went back to Henderson and they walked slowly across the tarmac, stopped and came back. They got into the truck with us and we drove miserably back.

Henderson slipped away to his room while the rest of us went through the motions of having tea. I don't know the best word to describe our emotions. Perhaps incredulity was uppermost. None of us had known her, and five years of total war had blunted everyone's sense of tragedy, yet there was something about the death of this unknown woman that we could not accept. Was it partly that we were so caught up in the Far Eastern campaign that we had forgotten the realities of life or death in the war in Europe, of which she was an indirect casualty? Or possibly that a traffic accident seemed cruelly banal? There was also the effect that this might have on all our plans for the operation. Quite apart from Henderson's personal anguish, the timing could not have been worse.

But only he and I knew about the poison pen letter and the misery it had caused him, however confidently he had agreed that it must be a hoax. The news of her death, coming so soon afterwards, must be heart-breaking. For all his cool and contained manner there was no lack of fire and susceptibility within. Could he still measure up to the emotional demands of his taxing role?

He came out and joined us, looking not so much stunned as drugged. "You know what's happened. I'd rather not talk about it. Not yet. Perhaps in a few days, if we survive this affair, I'd like to. I want you to know that this isn't going to change anything we do. So can we please go on as usual? That would help me a lot. I believe the latest airfield photos have come. Can we have a look at them?"

We pored over them but they showed no significant change, except for two bombers apparently waiting to take off. It was still astonishing that so little was happening at so important an airfield.

Henderson said that he was going for a walk but would be back in time for the General; I for one had forgotten all about his visit. I watched as he wandered off along the edge of the field, past the nubile women and round the corner of the woods.

We gathered in the big room. The table had been laid impressively, with napkins folded into water lilies and a curious floral extravaganza in the centre. From the kitchen came continuous excited chatter and a powerful smell of garlic and spices. Lewis presided over a tray of drinks. We helped ourselves and made conversation. Coe was immaculately turned out, decorations and all, and Buisman wore his RAF battledress with 'NEDERLAND' on the shoulders. The rest of us passed muster. There was no sign of Henderson. Then the jeep came up the track with Preston driving and the General beside him.

This was the first time that the rest of us had seen him close to. He was sturdy and unpretentious and had a reputation for honesty and fairness. As failure in Burma slowly turned to success he was generous in his praise for those who served under him. If there were delays and defeats it was the commanding officers that he sacked, when appropriate, instead of issuing reprimands to others through them. A reputation like his builds up more slowly than that of a flashier, publicity-seeking general – I name no names – but it lasts longer.

Preston introduced each of us to him separately. He didn't hog the conversation, nor expect to have his views reverently deferred to, but put the occasional shrewd question – not as a trap – and really listened to the answer, however lame. It seemed that he actually expected to learn something even from a group of junior officers. Henderson at last arrived, with apologies, seeming much as usual, though possibly even more laconic.

Adur entered, in his smartest mess jacket and pagri, to announce that dinner was ready, and the General delighted him by exchanging greetings. The ever-smiling Hira Lal hovered nearby.

There were seven of us. Preston, in the chair, presided at one end with the General on his right and Henderson on his left. Further down Buisman and Coe faced each other – more tranquilly now, I thought – and Taylor and I were the bottom pair. The cook had risen to his greatest heights: a soup of local vegetables was followed by an unidentified but palatable fish, and then a lavish curry with all the proper side dishes.

"I told him not to make it too hot," Preston explained, "because we didn't want to be gasping like fishes tonight and *hors de combat* tomorrow."

At first the talk was patchy. The General recounted some of the more bizarre effects of our unpreparedness in Burma. One anti-tank battery was equipped with guns made in Austria early in the century, captured by the Italians in 1918, recaptured by us in the Western Desert in 1942, and shipped out to Burma as a place that deserved nothing better. There survived barely a hundred rounds of ammunition for each gun, after which they became, as he said, literally museum pieces.

Hira Lal cleared the plates away and Adur carried in the cook's masterpiece, a gigantic iced cake with the Fourteenth Army crest on it, in the General's honour. We disposed of most of this, following it with coffee, and then the General asked Preston, as Mess President, if he might contribute a bottle which he had brought to mark the occasion. It proved to be Taylors' '27 port, which he had nursed on his lap on the journey and which Lewis, anxiously watched, opened and poured with great solemnity. It was an exceptional wine, and after the loyal toast we sipped it as the conversation became more serious. The General led off.

"Lewis, stop hovering and come and sit down with us. Gentlemen, you know that I became caught up with this matter right from the start, and that Colonel Preston has watched over it on my behalf since then. We both believe that it is not just an ingenious scheme but a practical proposition. If it had stood only an outside chance of success I would have cancelled it some way back, not out of tender-heartedness but because failure would have made their crypto system harder still to break. They would have recognised its vulnerability and taken steps to remedy it.

"We think your chances are distinctly better than evens. As a dispassionate observer I put them at two to one in your favour. The Supremo has also given it his official and personal blessing. We rate you, as a team, pretty high, and I can now tell you that I approve of the inclusion of every single one of you in it. That's why I've brought my last bottle to baptise the operation.

"But you know that this must be a job for volunteers. So I ask any of you who wish to withdraw to say so this evening, with my assurance that such a step would not in any way count against you."

I could hear Buisman's watch ticking in the silence.

"There's another aspect that I must touch on, painful though it is. As you know, Henderson has had sad news from home. I've offered to pluck him out of the operation and fly him home at once on compassionate grounds, and he has refused. I think he must have a second chance to consider it."

Henderson looked directly at him. "I'm grateful, sir. I have thought about it, but I could do no good by going to England. It would take several days to get there, and relatives and friends will have done everything necessary by then. They will understand. If anything I'm more determined than ever to see this through. Please count me in."

"I understand. Has anyone any personal question or reservation? This is your last chance to withdraw."

A long silence. None of us dared to look at the others.

"Very well. I thank you all. Preston, I think we had better have those detestable little forms that start 'I understand the risks …' for everyone to sign, and then that business will be out of the way."

Preston had them ready. We read the prosaic statement and signed.

"While we're at it I might as well tell you that Colonel Preston and Sergeant Lewis have been pestering me from the start to have them in the team too. I've had to put my foot down, not for the first time. As for the vexed question of who is to lead the team, I fancy that has solved itself but I shall maintain a discreet silence over the details. Colonel Preston will enlighten you in due course."

I tried to read some unspoken comment in his quizzical expression, but failed.

"I wish to thank our American and Netherlands friends for joining this versatile international group. I understand we have three pilots, three navigators, three Japanese linguists and five sharpshooters in a team of five. That must constitute some sort of record.

"Now I want to give you some more insight into the decision facing us in Burma. As everything else in this operation is Top Secret I shan't labour the point that this is too. We've pushed the enemy back but that's not enough. We need to knock him out before the monsoon puts paid to practically all movement. With Kawabe in charge I knew they would try to stand and fight north of the Irrawaddy. He was sacked for letting us beat him. With Kimura I'm not so sure. He may decide to make his stand on the far side. *I must know that.* Wherever his main position is, we're going to put a hook round it. The route for that hook will depend on knowing Kimura's plans. You know the map. If I send my men, trucks and tanks down the wrong valley they won't be able to get themselves over into the right one in time and without raising the alarm. Then the whole plan will collapse.

"That's where you come in. If you can trick them into keeping that crypto source open for a few more months or even weeks, that will tell us all we want to know, and we shall almost certainly win the Burma campaign before the May monsoon arrives. That's why we are backing you lot to the hilt. That's also the end of the pep talk. I think, Preston, that there's enough in that bottle for a toast?"

Preston filled the glasses himself and the General raised his. "To a fruitful Paperchase.

"Now I must get back to Comilla. Before I leave, it's time that we told you our little secret. We kept it dark so as to have a more relaxed evening, and in any case the business of volunteering had to be cleared up first."

I caught Henderson's eye. We knew what was coming next.

"Colombo have sent me a signal to say that Wallace and Lee dropped safely yesterday and sent off your signal to Rangoon about 1320 today. On my way here I heard that Rangoon had confirmed at 1800. So the whole thing is sewn up. You will fly to Agartala tomorrow and do Paperchase the next day. So get moving, and good luck."

He shook hands with us all. Soon afterwards the jeep roared down the track, and fifteen minutes later there was the noise of a plane taking off from the airfield.

DAY SEVEN:
FINISHING TOUCHES

The truck turned up early and Lewis drove us over to Doranda, a small town dominated by a large military hospital, leaving Preston behind. A banner hung across the main street, bearing the Congress Party badge and the message 'GO HOME, BRITISH'. A group of white-clothed youths shook their fists and shouted as we drove in. The hospital sentry directed us to the Leprosy Wing, where an RAMC doctor checked our identity and reassured us.

"This place is 100 per cent free of leprosy. No cases for over a year. It's handy for odd jobs like yours. I'm handing you over to Sen Gupta and John Srivastava but I'll be around and you'll each have a thorough medical inspection while you're here. Most of my patients don't change colour so dramatically.

"I understand that you want some chloroform and hints on using it for an unwilling passenger? I see I shall have to swallow my Hippocratic oath for a while." He rummaged on a shelf. "Use this pad, soak it quickly with the bottle when your patient needs it, and put it over his nose and mouth. Remove it as soon as he goes limp. Then put it where it won't make you pass out too, in case he wakes up first."

We walked through the bare echoing rooms and began by having casual haircuts 'to remove European characteristics', as Srivastava put it. Then a shower, and after drying ourselves we each took a dip in lukewarm khaki dye.

"Please to put head right underneath," said Sen Gupta. He rubbed the dye into the scalp to remove any telltale patches.

"Now one again, please. Next you must go into that warm room and dry without any using of towel."

I asked him what was in the dye bath.

"Ah. That is secret recipe, but I can tell you that walnut juice is important constituency."

Buisman and Taylor were already half dry and I joined them. Srivastava, plump and methodical, came through with a small foot-bath of dye.

"Please let me apply more to soles of feet. When you are walking about here you are always removing dye. Ah, you European men are so ticklish there. Do not worry; it is enough. Now we have final session with facial cosmetics in view. Some of you are having ruddy cheek. Not at all Oriental fashion."

I was afraid that Taylor might make some clumsy joke about Buisman needing less dye than the rest of us. Fortunately he didn't. There was a mild but not unpleasant stinging sensation, and in the mirror we looked like muddy ghosts. Finally, hair and eyebrows had to be dyed, using a different formula to produce the raven black gloss. When that was done they gave each of us a searching scrutiny and that was that. Coffee was on its way over and we practised slurping it in the Japanese style.

I wondered what the doctor would say about my attack of malaria. He shrugged. "Normally you'd be in bed where we can keep an eye on you. I know if I suggest that I'll be overruled by your mad Colonel, so I can only tell you to go on with the mepacrine, check your temperature if you feel really bad, and concentrate on what matters, or you may doze off. Then you go straight into hospital as soon as you're back. On that understanding I'll pass you."

Lewis returned to collect us, raised his eyebrows at our appearance but refrained from comment. He ushered us into the back of the truck and made sure that the canvas concealed us, both when we drove out of the gates and when we reached the Gurkha post. Obviously they had orders to let the load through unexamined.

Adur and Hira Lal witnessed our arrival. Adur took it quite calmly but Hira Lal seemed stunned. Taylor took me on one side.

"I'm worried about Henderson. Have you seen his eyes? There's a wild look as if he was going to burst into flames. And he spent a long time with the Doc just now. This mission is going to take a hell of a lot out of him. Is he really fit for it?"

I had noticed it too. He had seemed uncharacteristically short-tempered that morning. But what could we do? He'd been thoroughly checked over. I'd be no good in his role and there was no time to start recruiting for a stand-in. We agreed to do all we could to keep him on an even keel despite his personal tragedy. Yet if we did that too obviously we might make things worse. He was not a man to appreciate being cosseted.

Now we had to be photographed in our Jap flying kit. An Army photographer did the whole job on the spot, and the prints were pasted into very convincing identity cards, specially forged for us in Delhi. I became 'MIYAGUCHI, HIDEKUNI, Colonel, born at Nagoya.' Henderson was 'YAMAJI, TOSHIAKI, Major-General …' – and so on. Finally Preston wielded a heavy stamp across the corner of each photograph and I scribbled a different illegible signature on each card, and they were complete. We aged them with a grubby cloth and added creases and dog-ears. The face that stared at me from my pass was unrecognisable, yet when I looked in the mirror I saw, logically enough, that it was now mine. The transformation was absolute. Our team consisted of a group of typical Japanese officers.

We soon discovered what Preston and Lewis had been up to while we were at Doranda. The spare room had heavy shutters bolted across the windows and steel wardrobes installed, one for each of us. Into these went all our kit and personal possessions, including rings and watches. There were Jap watches, binoculars and sunglasses for us all and an array of boots, uniforms and peaked caps. Only some of these would be needed during the flight, when flying kit and flying helmets would envelop us, but it was thought prudent to have them with us. The insignia of rank fitted on easily, and under them we hid the little suicide tablets. I didn't care for the way Henderson examined his. Finally we took over rows of medal ribbons anonymously bequeathed to us and appropriate to our new rank. His were quite spectacular: three rows in all and vividly coloured.

"Swords will not be worn," Preston had decreed. "A terrible nuisance in a plane, and the Japanese ones are long and awkward. But I'll show General Yamaji how to carry his. He ought to have it handy for the sake of appearance. But are you all positive that you have no personal papers or diaries in your new kit?"

Adur knocked at the door and came in, looking worried. "Excuse me, Colonel sahib. Hira Lal run away. After he see gentlemen come back he say he not feeling well, will go for lie down on charpoy. Just now I go look for him to make ready for serving lunch, but he already take his t'ings and run away."

Preston frowned and sent Lewis out in the jeep. He returned ten minutes later. "Nowhere in sight, sir, and he didn't go out past the guard post."

"Damnation. Get hold of that signalman. Get a call out to all units in the Ranchi area, plus the civvy police, to look out for him and pull him in. Get me the Military Police after that."

While he waited for the call he discussed the disappearance with Adur. Nothing seemed to be missing, nor had there been anything to arouse suspicion. Hira Lal had not been seen trying our doors or peering into our windows, and no unusual visitors had been noticed.

"But he too sweet, sahib. He too nice than possible. Good he go."

"I'm going to give those Gurkhas a rocket. They should have seen him sneaking off if they'd been on their toes. He must have slipped out through the wood. Once he was over the hill to Patratu he could catch a bus to anywhere he chose."

Coe added, "Once or twice I thought he was gumshoeing around behind us when we were talking business. But whenever I thought about it, there wasn't anything that would make sense security-wise."

Taylor had been going through his clutch of maps. "Has anyone seen the north Burma sheet?" he asked sheepishly. "We were working on it yesterday. I had it first thing this morning."

"I trust you didn't take it to the hospital?"

"No. I left it in my room."

"Which of course you kept locked?"

"I-I can't swear to it, sir. I generally do."

Preston snorted. "Lewis, fetch Adur for me."

"Adur, was Taylor sahib's room locked this morning?"

Adur looked unhappy. "No, sir. While you getting ready store-room I go check all doors. That door not locked, so I lock him."

"You were quite right."

An uncomfortable silence as Adur withdrew.

"You can never trust the natives," Buisman muttered sardonically. "Leave it to the White Man."

"Hou je mond, jongen!" Preston said furiously. "Taylor, had you and Coe cleared up the working notes you made on that chart?"

Taylor reddened. Coe cleared his throat. "No, sir. We were planning on doing that about now."

"And what do they show?"

"Sir, we pencilled in the southern half of the Agartala-Cox's Bazaar leg, and the start of the next stretch."

"No timings or other choice details shown?"

"No, sir. Definitely not."

"Thank God for that. So to summarise: the marked chart showing that significant part of our plans was left in your unlocked room for several hours, Taylor? Despite my instructions that rooms should be locked? And the one member of the domestic staff whom we know least about absconded, possibly with the map, soon after seeing our party in enemy disguise. Does that seem a happy coincidence, you clown?"

"I'm terribly sorry, sir. Is there anything I can do …?"

"Make yourself scarce for a while. You may have to face a court-martial for negligence if the operation goes wrong as a result. Go and make sure nothing else is missing. What about the air photos of Mingaladon? Coe, you go and check with him. Thoroughly, mind. No cover-up."

When he got through to the MPs' commanding officer he gave him the gist of Hira Lal's abrupt departure. "No, I don't have anything specific, but I don't like the way this chap decamped exactly when we have something rather hush-hush going on here, and I dare not discount the possibility of the theft of Top Secret material. Can you put a check on telephone calls? No, I don't mean all of them. Are there any local Congress Party extremists? What about the Subhas Chandra lot? And please warn Calcutta too. I'm grateful. Jim."

"It's a lesson to me," he said almost plaintively. "It's no use saying I didn't like the look of him. Plenty of fine fellows fall under that heading. But I shouldn't have run even an outside risk. I'll have to break the news to the General next."

The General was down in Arakan, but his Number Two promised to check on local security and especially on any recent reports of Indian revolutionaries. Back in our days of retreat and defeat they had been a real danger. The turn of the tide, coupled with their rapid disillusionment about the benefits a Japanese victory would actually bring, had led to a partial collapse, but some of them could still pose a local security threat.

A truck drew up outside and two RAF corporals arrived to equip us with parachutes and explain how to use them in an emergency. As much of our flight would be over water, each parachute was combined with a dinghy pack and a CO_2 bottle to inflate it with, placed so that we should have to sit on it uncomfortably for hours on end. We persuaded them that this was not just unnecessary but an obstacle to our fighting efficiency, so we had to practise putting the whole thing on in a hurry. They took our outlandish appearance in their stride, but when Preston saw us lumbering along with these bundles bumping behind us, he guffawed. "You look like ducks waddling down to a pond. Where's that photographer?" He seemed to have recovered his spirits.

That was the last hurdle to clear. The wardrobes were locked and the room padlocked, one key with Preston, one with Lewis. Adur, still worrying over Hira Lal's vanishing trick, had lunch ready. His buxom daughter, whom we had glimpsed on her journeys between house and kitchen, helped to serve in his place. Her eyes were usually downcast, but from time to time she flashed us a quick un-demure smile as she whisked empty plates away. "She not afraid, now she know who you are," her father explained. Taylor toyed with the first course, made excuses and left. We packed our new kit, bade Adur farewell and drove off. The Gurkhas were staying on duty, patrolling the area and guarding the rest-house, until Operation Paperchase was over.

At the airfield the plane had been pulled out of the hangar, the engines run up and tested, and moved to a far corner. All seven of us clambered to our places, joined by an air-gunnery instructor who had been sworn to secrecy. A final pre-flight check and we were off.

The first part of our run to Agartala was tedious and uneventful, and we gave Calcutta a wide berth by flying out to sea near Cuttack for our rendezvous with the target-towing aircraft. The target drogue, a conical canvas sleeve towed behind the plane, would give us good elementary practice since it couldn't go as fast as a Zero fighter.

"Align that sighting ring on the target and swing the gun as it comes past. Watch the tracer bullets to see where your shots are going. Always aim further forward than you think. Keep your shoulder hard against the butt, and aim the gun by swinging on your feet. First run, Joe," he called on the radio.

The target plane came diving past. "*Wait for it.* We're not popular if we hit the plane. Here comes the target. Wait. Ready? Fire."

A rattling din as I fired, but most of the shorts were wildly out.

"Next run, Joe."

This time I did better, and the third time, remembering to hold the gun hard into my shoulder, I peppered it quite well. Then Henderson had his turn, and knowing him to be a first-class shot I expected him to do better. To my surprise he missed on every run and swore luridly for the first time since I'd known him.

Finally Buisman fired the big 20-mm cannon from the power-driven turret above us. His experience told. Most of the shells found their mark and the drogue collapsed and floated limply down into the Bay of Bengal. The instructor raised his voice in mock anger. "That target was the property of the Royal Air Force. How shall I break the news when I get back? Seriously, that was pretty shooting. I'll personally check and load all the guns at Agartala. Good luck to you."

Buisman was delighted. Unlike the rest of us he felt our mission to be a crusade or vendetta, with killing Japanese as the main objective. Every day he sharpened the short Malay *kris*, with its wicked wavy blade, that he carried in a sheath under his bush-jacket, and I knew he was itching for an excuse to use it at Mingaladon.

We were now running in over the easternmost part of the Sundarbans, the Ganges estuary as big as Wales. As everybody said, Agartala was a dump, usually hot and humid, and a depressing contrast with Ranchi. It was also a busy RAF station, with Beaufighters and Dakotas of several squadrons coming and going.

Taylor was glad to be given clearance to land from the south-west, because the north-east end of the runway had a notorious dip which they never seemed to have time to fill, and this could form a hazardous switchback. We were directed to taxi straight to a hangar which would be guarded overnight. A truck whisked us off to a group of small tents and one larger mess tent, all in a security area newly roped off and guarded. It was like being in a zoo, this feeling of isolation, so different from the welcome received at a well-established unit. But a party of five Japanese officers, even if escorted by a British colonel and a sergeant, would hardly have been welcome in the mess.

Two RAF officers from Comilla were waiting to check the final flight details with Preston. They looked uneasy.

"What's your trouble, Bob?"

"There's a signal just in from ALFSEA, sir, that's bound to make you see red."

"I thought the egregious Agnew had thrown in the sponge. Tell me the worst. Where is it?"

He goggled at it.

"My God. 'RECOMMEND SERIOUSLY CONSIDER RAF ESCORT TO RANGOON OR NEAR STOP AGNEW'. Is he out of his mind? One hint that we had an RAF escort would settle our fate. Perhaps he really means a Japanese escort? Could we invite him to arrange that? Please get him on the blower at once."

He paced up and down, gently fuming. "Does that son-of-a-bitch never quit?" Coe wanted to know.

"Is that you, Agnew? Where is he? Out of reach? I'm not surprised. Kindly note this reply to his signal, from Colonel Preston, and pass it to him without delay. Can you hear? It's a shocking line. 'SLIM FORBIDS NEW RAF PLAN'. Got it? All right, I'll spell it."

He drew a deep breath.

'SLIM: Senseless, Lunatic, Idiotic, Maniacal. FORBIDS: Farcical, Obtuse, Ridiculous, Blockheaded, Imbecile – um – Doltish, Stupid. NEW: Nonsensical, Empty-headed, Witless. RAF: Rubbishy, Asinine, Fatuous. PLAN: Let me think – Pigheaded, Lunatic, Addle-pated, Numbskull. Message ends. You send that along to him at top speed, if you please." He set down the phone with the flourish of a concert pianist executing the final curlicue of a showy cadenza. "The effrontery, the sheer gall of the fellow. To dream up a cockeyed scheme like that at the eleventh hour, having absented himself from all our planning and disgraced himself on the trial run …"

"Not a favourite of yours, sir?"

He subsided. "How did you guess? Let's see the rest of the agenda."

The other news was straightforward. The latest weather reports, drawn from our own sources and the intercepted Japanese signals, spoke of mainly clear weather over the Bay of Bengal and southern Burma. But though the worst of the monsoon was over, there was still monsoon cloud in central and north Burma, which we would miss on the way out but might meet on the way back. Were we sure, they asked, that we couldn't use the same route both ways, via the big loop?

"No. Even with the extra tank there's not much in hand – even if all goes smoothly. If it doesn't we'll be eating into our reserves. Nothing doing."

A south-east sea wind was now expected, so we ought to allow extra time for the outward flight – perhaps as much as an hour. We discussed this. Whatever happened we must not arrive at Mingaladon early. No waiting for the Major or anyone else. Dead on time at 1315, or possibly a little later, would be fine. We compromised. "We'll put the first stage back thirty minutes, leave here at 0730, arrive Cox's Bazaar 0830, leave there 0930 and still plan to touch down at Mingaladon 1315–1330. Will you fix this end for us?"

"Agreed. What about the return flight?"

"We fixed with your AOC that we'll transmit 7272 plus our estimated position when we're nearly in escort range, say about 500 miles out. Apart from that we'll keep radio silence. Explain to them that if any Jap aircraft spot us with an RAF escort they'll smell a rat at once. So the escort needs to destroy them, not just drive them off, or they may whistle up more Zeros."

"I'll tell them. Finally these diversionary attacks: no changes?"

"You'd better recap."

(See map on page 154 for the rest of Operation Paperchase.)

"One: we attack Akyab and Ramree airfields, the two furthest north, 0930–0945 as you leave Cox's Bazaar. Two: attack the next three, Cheduba, Sandoway and Bassein, 1215–1230, soon before you reach Mingaladon. We also raid three inland airfields, including Prome and Toungoo, to confuse the pattern. How does that strike you, sir?"

"Only one thing I'm not happy about: those coastal raids point straight towards Mingaladon. Cancel one of them, the least important, and do the rest in reverse order, south to north."

"Easy. Joe, scrub Sandoway and do Bassein, Cheduba, Ramree and Akyab. And of course all RAF, USAF and Chinese Air Force crews are being briefed about your existence and suspicious markings. So are coastal units and naval vessels. Does that cover the lot? Tell us the whole story when you get back."

They gave us the latest Mingaladon photos. No aircraft were on the runway, but nearby were ten Zero fighters neatly drawn up.

Nothing very surprising, but where had they been before and why were they there now? Waiting for us? It was no use worrying now.

We dined in the big mess tent with its walls brailed up to let in such fresh air as Agartala could provide. The local belief was that if you slept inside a mosquito net it kept the breeze out but let the Agartala mosquitoes in, so none of us used one. I was still queasy but I was past the shivery stage and felt sure that at this rate I should last out. Any mosquito that bit me would die of an overdose of mepacrine.

Our attempts at casual conversation were a complete flop. Each of us knew that tomorrow we should either be celebrating or dead. If the latter, we hoped it would be mercifully swift. "The Last Supper?" Taylor whispered ghoulishly in my ear. Damn his graveyard humour. Preston had given up trying to jolly us along. Although, like Lewis, he was not in the team, he was as closely absorbed in it as we were, and it still irked him that he could not take part.

Henderson broke the spell. "I've had a Shakespeare quotation going round my head all day. Do you mind if I recite it? It won't cheer us up much but it might exorcise the evil spirits. You reminded me of it when you quoted the lines about Banquo's ghost the other day. Macbeth speaks it just before he murders Duncan, and perhaps it fits our case."

He began, "'Is this a dagger which I see before me, the handle toward my hand?'" and finished, "'It is a knell that summons thee to heaven or to hell.'"

Buisman ran his fingers agitatedly through his hair. "Now you open my eyes a little bit wider. Any of us with wives and children, how do you think we will sleep tonight, heh? You know I don't forget them even without that drama. I have to leave them behind in Sumatra, and nobody hears one damn thing about them since two and half years ago. Are they together, and are they alive? The Japanese do terrible things to them, that's all we know. When the Germans bomb Rotterdam to pieces, all the schoolchildren in

Netherlands and in East Indies stand up and say, 'Wij zijn niet bang' – we are not afraid. But I tell you I am afraid. Only a fool is not afraid of tomorrow." He stared defiantly round at us. "And all is for a crazy book of numbers. Don't worry that I will pull out. I think of Anneke with Paula and Doritje and I pretend I am not afraid."

The quiet spectral intensity of Henderson's voice had been chilling, yet I think he was right: putting our fears into words dispelled some of them. Nobody else wanted to talk much and soon afterwards we turned in early.

In the middle of the airless night I woke and realised that the line 'And take the present horror from the time,' had been relentlessly marching and counter-marching through my head. I had the present horrors all right: that I would be panic-stricken at some decisive moment and be unable to do or say the one vital thing. But I couldn't pull out, any more than Buisman or the others; the single fear of being judged a coward eclipsed the rest.

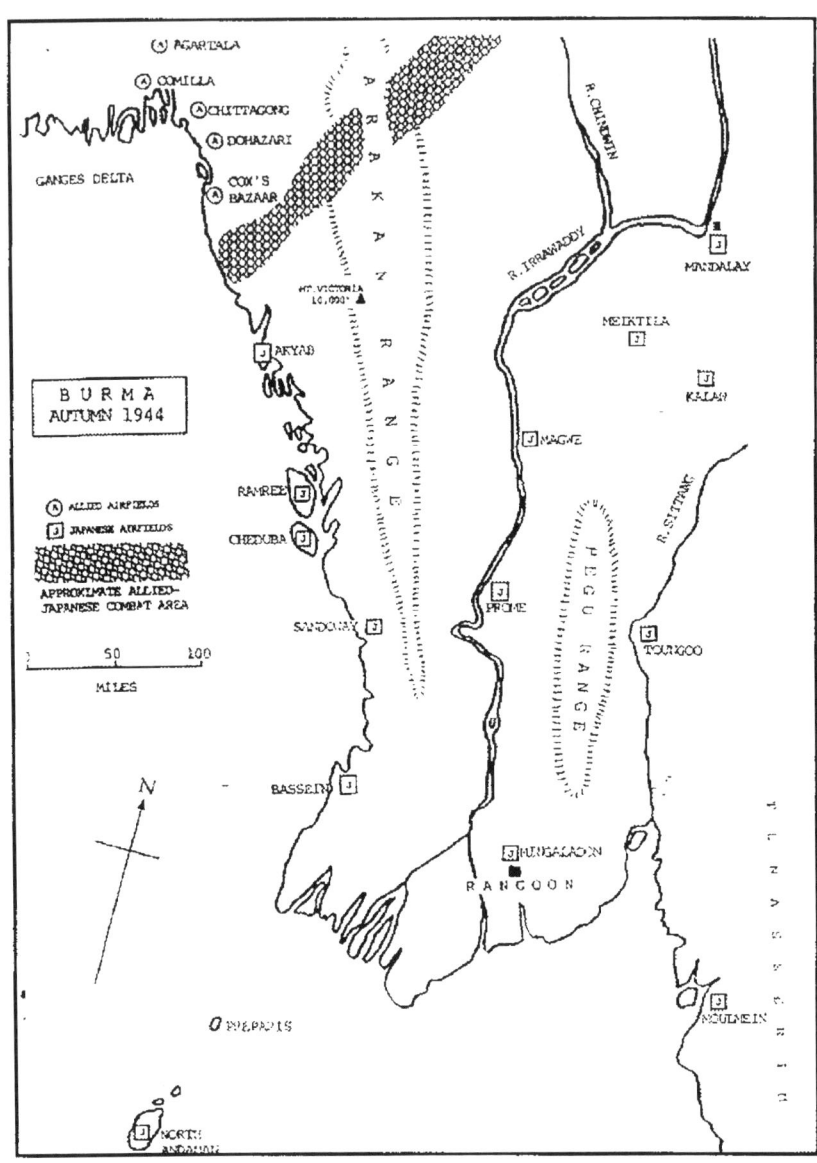

Map of Burma, Autumn 1944

DAY EIGHT:
OPERATION PAPERCHASE

I was woken by Lewis at 0600 hrs: there was tea in the mess tent. I had a quick wash and walked over to meet the others. Communal early tea was a novelty, though welcome in this swampy climate, so some of us were shaven and others not. Preston was swathed in a stunning Chinese silk dressing gown, electric blue but bearing on its back a large black dragon with a scarlet face and yellow talons. He pirouetted coquettishly for our benefit. "You likee velly lucky Frying Dlagon? It's the best I could do to wish you luck. The forecast is the same, so don't be tempted to change any plans. Come and have breakfast as soon as you're ready."

All around engines were being run up ready for the day's operations, most of which had nothing to do with us. Preston radiated a celestial calm; we might have been getting ready for a picnic. Henderson seemed exactly as usual, but still with that worrying intensity just below the surface. Would he be able to play his demanding part as the Japanese General? That reminded me: in my role as Colonel Miyaguchi I had to hand over the receipt to the genuine Major at Mingaladon. I patted my pocket to make sure it was there.

"Now," said Preston, "I have two things to tell you. The first you'll have guessed some time ago. Calcutta have obviously abandoned any idea of nominating a successor to the unfortunate Colonel Agnew, so Henderson will be in charge as we always planned. The second is a confession, and I owe it to you to make it now. Agnew's airsickness on the trial flight was no accident. I judged it would be disastrous for him to lead this mission, so I got Adur to make up an old-fashioned irritant, well known hereabouts. I wondered about chopped tiger-whiskers, widely used around the North-West frontier, but he warned me that they might be fatal. I stressed that it must be just enough to make him decidedly uncomfortable for the flight, and no more. Adur mixed this magic potion into Agnew's portion of the breakfast curry, which was hot enough to cover any odd flavour. I think it would be prudent not to enlighten Agnew. I trust you will keep our little secret?"

He looked almost woebegone, yet we were all laughing helplessly when the truck arrived. We were leaving nothing behind, and had already put on our flying kit, so there was only our personal equipment to take with us. Preston and Lewis climbed in too and we drove round to our plane. We put our things on board, and then out of nowhere a jeep arrived with the General sitting beside his driver.

It really was good of him to come and see us off. He had watched over our plan from the start and given it his powerful backing which had opened doors and removed obstacles all along the way. And here we were, five Allied officers in disguise climbing into a captured Japanese bomber resplendent in its war paint on a muggy morning, with a fateful day ahead.

"No farewell speeches," he assured us. "I came to make sure Preston and Lewis weren't stowing away." All three of them shook hands with us and wished us luck. The General looked at his watch. "Better check yours. It's exactly 0715, which is local Japanese time too. Off you go."

It no longer felt strange to climb in and find our places, but it always took a while to get used to the mixed smells of aviation fuel, paint and fug. Our flying suits felt clammy and the perspex windows steamed up as the low sun warmed the fuselage. The RAF sergeant slammed the hatch and Buisman locked it from inside. Taylor and Coe sorted out their maps. Taylor gestured to the trolley-man to start the port engine, and it jerked into life. Then Coe gestured from his side and the starboard one started. The trolley and chocks were pulled away. We gave a last wave to the small group on the tarmac as we trundled round to the runway.

We had priority to take off. The engines were tested to maximum revs, and then we were on the move, the tail came up, and we were off. Agartala dropped away, a loose spoon rattled in someone's lunch-bag, and Taylor banked the plane round as we slowly climbed. The airfield dwindled and became lost. He banked more steeply and there was that absurd phenomenon again: we stayed level while the vast arc of brownish plain tilted up on our left, mottled with trees, rivers and swamps.

As always the big engines seemed to strain to take us up, and the vibration spread along the whole fuselage. Groans, rattles and squeaks that I had not noticed before formed a mechanical counterpoint above the steady bass drone of the airscrews. There were more air pockets this morning, and in each one you could feel the aircraft and most of your body sink while your stomach flew on in a straight line. Someone's voice on the intercom said, "Poor old Agnew."

Our first leg took us between the Chin foothills to the east and the delta of the Ganges and Brahmaputra rivers, stretching away in a maze of channels and sandbanks, to the west. On our left was a dazzling white beach; the lower hills were cinnamon and the Arakan mountains a vibrant blue-green. We flew over Chittagong and Dohazari airfields, home ground to Taylor, and began to lose height to put down at Cox's Bazaar.

The runway there had been steadily lengthened throughout the Arakan campaigns. We had what the pilots called a firm landing and we called a thud. The plane rumbled along to the refuelling bowser. Here we had to fill every tank up to the brim, checking not by gauge but by eye. No leaks? Tyres and brakes OK? All control surfaces working smoothly? Certainly our Japanese markings caused the ground crew, despite their careful briefing and tight security, a good deal of thought.

The take-off run seemed endless. The full load of fuel weighed us down, and it was a relief when the skinny trees at the end of the runway flashed underneath. The undercarriage came up with a slow growl and a final clank. As we began climbing we noticed unusual activity below, with Spitfires taking off singly and racing off towards the south-east. We soon turned on oxygen and suit heaters and climbed towards our ceiling of over 30,000 feet. We turned west and settled down for the long flight.

Our course swept us well out into the Bay of Bengal to keep clear of any patrolling Japanese aircraft, and then well south of Rangoon. So although the direct route to Rangoon is little over 400 miles, our detour put it up to 900. At our cruising speed of 250 m.p.h. this would be a three-and-a-half-hour flight, most of which should be uneventful. The sky was clear with cotton-wool blobs of cloud below us, each with its own shadow on the sea, which was otherwise almost invisible. The pilots had their sunglasses on because the sun made a great dazzling reflection ahead. My thoughts ranged over the week at Ranchi, the day ahead, my family and friends. Nothing seemed real. Even the aircraft's progress was marked only by the hubbub of the engines, the creaking of the fuselage, and disjointed quacking overheard on the intercom. We were suspended in our dream world.

A radio signal started coming in and after a minute Buisman gave it to me. It was in the special cipher I had constructed for our trip, and I deciphered it quickly: 'ENEMY TRIED BIG RAID COXS BAZAAR 0945 STOP RARITY NOWADAYS STOP LEAK OR COINCIDENCE QUERY NO RPT NO WARNING FROM WEC RPT WEC STOP BOOK CHANGED QUERY PONDER IMPLICATIONS STOP PRESS ON REGARDLESS QUERY PRESTON ENDS'.

Henderson and I agreed that both questions were acutely worrying. If we had not altered our timings the previous evening, we should have been on the ground refuelling at 0945. If that meant a security leak, what sort of reception could we expect at Mingaladon?

He pointed out that if Hira Lal *had* stolen Taylor's map and passed it on to some network of agents, they might have linked it – and our disguise, which had so worried him – with our flights from Ranchi in a blatantly Japanese aircraft, and made a shrewd guess at our destination. But they could never have learnt our original timings, which we had never put in writing.

I thought that even if they had, Cox's Bazaar would have been the last place where they would try to intercept us. Its fighter and flak defences were well known. They would have waited till we flew into their clutches at Rangoon. That might still happen, of course.

The other point was this: our breaking of the 2244 code at WEC sometimes gave us warning of enemy air raids, so if this one came out of the blue it might be tempting to assume that they had changed to the new book. That had been on the cards for weeks. It would be just our luck if they had switched to it today. If so our Major Hashimoto, the man in charge locally, would be the last person to hand it over. The whole bogus story would stink to high heaven. It would also sign our death warrant.

But I explained to Henderson that most of the tactical signals weren't on 2244 but on BULBUL, a different crypto system that often defeated us. There was no proper evidence that the new 2244 book was in use.

There was no time to consult the others. Preston would be hopping on one leg until he heard from us. We agreed to treat the whole thing as coincidence, take the risk and go ahead. He said to Buisman, "Send a short series of dots to say 'Yes'. Nothing else. Check that they acknowledge, and that's that."

But it was one thing to make the decision and another to disregard the possible implications. I could sense that he was thinking the same. We should be walking a tightrope at Mingaladon.

We rummaged in our lunch bags, filled with captured Japanese rations on which we had already had some practice. Coffee was common to both sides, and the thermos flasks were also Japanese, but captured toilet paper showed uncommon thoroughness.

We flew over Preparis South Channel, some eighty miles clear of North Andaman. The whole archipelago had been raided by the Navy in June, to suggest that we might be contemplating a seaborne assault on southern Burma and to keep in this area troops which could otherwise have been used to fight against us in Burma. We hoped these activities had not put the island garrisons on the alert, and kept our eyes skinned as we passed between tiny Preparis Island and the main group of islands. At our ceiling it would be no surprise if we slipped past unobserved. It looked as if we were in luck.

But from now on everything would be trickier. Soon we must assume the role of a Jap aircraft flying north from Singapore to Rangoon, and we must do that rapidly yet without arousing suspicion. Our course took us close to the Tenasserim coast, the long sliver of Burma that runs down parallel with part of Thailand. That was the Jap route, sensibly near their coastal airfields. We had to lose height as well.

Now we were due south of Rangoon, still heading east but about to turn north. "Bangkok straight ahead," said Buisman jokingly. He had known it before the war and looked forward to seeing it again one day, but the joke misfired. Twenty minutes to go, and we were flying blindly into a box, with the enemy on three sides and our own progress inexorably closing the door behind us. The fear of a trap, cleverly set by ourselves, had always nagged at us. Now it suddenly became overwhelming. I remembered Preston's gaffe about Yamamoto's punctuality leading to his own destruction.

The sky above us clouded over as we turned north-east, then north, losing height to 15,000 feet and letting our speed fall away. At first we could see the pattern of waves, but cloud banks started to form and thicken below. Taylor, who knew the area from the days of our retreat two and a half years before, took over the controls again. Down to 10,000 feet, then 5,000, with views of a dark shoreline far ahead. Then we were in ragged clouds, bouncing vigorously in the cross-currents of stormy air.

I recalled the warning before our trial flight: "It's no good if everyone is airsick just when we reach Rangoon." Rain rattled on the windows. Tattered clouds raced past, with occasional glimpses of sea below. Down to 3,000, the plane creaking in the air pockets. Then we were in the ragged bottoms of the cloud banks, with small fishing craft below us along the muddy shores flanking the estuary that runs up to Rangoon. Ten minutes to go.

"Target straight ahead," called Taylor. "Landing drill, everybody. Remember those loosening-up exercises."

We checked that our firearms were ready and slung our binoculars round our necks, and stretched our cramped legs while we clung on to the fuselage struts and peered down. We swung a little west of north, crossing Elephant Point and running up the Rangoon River, now a treacly consistency. Syriam, still a colonial town along its main streets, crawled under our port wing, followed by a desolate tangle of creeks and a battered oil refinery, and suddenly there were pagodas everywhere, some of them gaunt and shabby but Shwe Dagon an astonishing array of spires round the tall pointed stupa, its golden sheets bright against sandy and red patterns around it. I chose this incongruous moment to recall the guide-book statistics: 9,000 sheets of solid gold covered the graceful tower, and the pinnacle held 5,000 jewels, with one 76-carat diamond crowning the very top.

Mingaladon airfield is just north of the city, in a low-lying area. We continued to lose height and speed over the nondescript suburbs until there was a criss-cross pattern of runways ahead, and the airfield opened out on both sides.

The forecast had predicted a light south-west wind here and the windsock confirmed it. We had agreed that we would do a leisurely circuit at 1,000 feet while we spied out the land. With flaps halfway down we circled over rice fields while three of us searched through our binoculars.

It looked extraordinarily quiet. Too quiet? But there was nothing to arouse our suspicions. The main runway was clear. If there had been any truckloads of troops nearby, we should have seen them. Yet the Japanese were notoriously good at ambushes. Nothing could be taken at its face value. No aircraft were moving, though several in various stages of repair were being worked on, just as in the reconnaissance photos. Ten or twelve Zero fighters were still drawn up where they had been in the last photograph, but there was no activity round them. None had their engines running nor even starter-trolleys nearby. Keep calm. Near the HQ buildings several cars and trucks were parked: natural enough. Buisman gave the thumbs-up sign. Henderson and I looked at each other and nodded.

"Nothing unusual in sight from the cockpit, pilots?"

"Nothing."

"Very well. Prepare to land. Everything from now on in Japanese."

The radio crackled and Coe said fluently, "Yes, General Yamaji's aircraft from Imperial HQ. Thank you."

Almost too good to be true. Keep calm. Flaps right down, undercarriage down.

'Three greens' from Coe: main wheels and tail wheel had locked down properly.

We took the last turn wide and began a long straight run in. Small huts and a run-down garage swept below our wheels, then the sewage works, then the perimeter fence. The runway rose to meet us. Taylor throttled right down, nudged the control column back, and very gently executed a perfect three-point landing. It was 1320, ten minutes before our deadline and five minutes late for the Major.

Henderson said in crisp idiomatic Japanese, "Take her right back to the far end near the windsock. Turn her round ready for take-off. Keep the engines ticking over."

All this had been agreed long before, but we were no longer pretending to be Japanese. We *were* Japanese.

"Very good, General," replied Coe.

We ran back along the taxiing track to the east end of the runway, turned and stopped just clear so that other aircraft could still use it but we could take off at once. The sun glared fitfully through thin sheets of pewter cloud, with a coppery glow to the west. It was hot and humid and I felt the sweat trickling down my back. Keep calm.

To our right and behind us lay paddy fields, and we had seen from the air that they could not harbour an ambush party. Straight ahead was a dilapidated factory, apparently deserted. Over to the left stretched the main area of the airfield and we continued to scan it through our glasses. There was no movement anywhere. I understood the cliché about time standing still.

It would have been eerie if all had been silent, but the big engines were purring steadily. At last a small open truck pulled away from the control tower area and headed round the perimeter track towards us. Buisman came down from his turret and slid open the port blister, letting in a cooling gale from that engine. Henderson and I had our holsters open and our automatics ready. Buisman picked up his machine-carbine and held it just out of sight. He pocketed two of the small grenades and undid his jacket to reach his dagger if need be. With his special hatred of the Japanese it would be the dagger, not the chloroform bottle, if he had the chance.

The truck moved very slowly. Was it meant to distract our attention from some assault party? Apparently not. There was only one man in the front of the truck and hardly room to hide anyone in the open space behind. But I felt that we were watching a film in which other people had written the script and played the main parts. At any moment all hell might break loose.

The starboard engine laboured for a few seconds before they revved it up. Henderson stood up and surveyed the scene grandly. His sunglasses, helped by the shadowing peak of his hat, kept his telltale blue eyes hidden. He had never looked more completely in control of himself.

The truck stopped some ten yards away and the driver stepped down. He was not a caricature Japanese but of medium height, with a neat moustache. He wore a floppy cap, boots and breeches, and a bush-jacket with Major's badges. I was glad to see that he was carrying a parcel of about the right size and was apparently unarmed. He drew himself up, marched towards us, halted below the open blister and saluted, standing sturdily in the slipstream. He looked a thoughtful, reasonable man, somehow less typically Japanese than Henderson now appeared.

Illogically I felt rising panic. I knew that whatever went wrong *I could not kill this man.* Inside my skull a macabre voice was whispering, "Do come and meet Mr Hashimoto from Japan, such a nice man and so interesting." I could no more shoot him, if he refused to hand the book over, than I could turn the gun on one of our own team. That was it: he had been drafted into the team without realising it. He knew his part.

Henderson waited, knowing that by Japanese military etiquette the junior officer speaks first. The Major, quite self-possessed, called above the noise of the engines, "*Shosho dono. Hashimoto de arimasu; hajimete o-meni kakarimasu.*" General, sir, I am Hashimoto. It is a pleasure (literally 'the first time') to see you.

"*Go-kuro datta,*" – well done – replied Henderson. "My password is TAKETORI. And yours?"

"Mine is TSURAYUKI, sir."

Now, after the pleasant overtures, the moment of truth.

"You may now give me the codebook, Major, and the certificate of destruction for our signal, if you please."

"Excuse me, Excellency," said Hashimoto tentatively. "There is a certain difficulty …"

My heart missed a beat. Were we going to have to fight for it after all? I heard Buisman breathing heavily just behind me. He had sensed that there was some hitch. Henderson seemed quite unmoved, and responded tolerantly enough. "What difficulty? Please explain quickly. We have no time to spare."

"Can there not be some identification? Your exalted message clearly stated the requirements, but my loyalty also demands that I should confirm the identity of the person to whom I hand over these documents – if you will forgive my presumption. The situation is a highly unusual one."

"A perfectly proper attitude, Hashimoto. I understand your position. Here is my identity card. Kindly satisfy yourself."

Hashimoto glanced at it quickly and, thank God, appeared convinced.

"Thank you, Excellency. Here is the codebook, and the signal destruction certificate."

He stretched up to give the parcel and the envelope to Henderson, who handed them to me fastidiously, as if it were below his dignity to look inside.

I unwrapped it as calmly as I could. Both sections of the book were there, and the reference number on the cover, 04-shiki R 70718, was correct. I opened the first book and flipped over some pages. This was not the one we knew so well. Likewise the second. I looked up 3267, one of the commonest code-groups in the old book since it meant both 'open brackets' and 'close brackets', and it had become 'airspeed indicator' – a rarity. Even the format of the printing was slightly different.

Out of the corner of my eye I saw Henderson gazing austerely across the airfield, and the Major not quite presuming to make conversation. I felt I had to check several more groups. All had new meanings. Yes, this was the new book. I could hardly believe it.

"*Machigai arimasen, shosho dono,*" I told Henderson. Everything is in order, General. I gave him our carefully forged receipt form, already signed.

"My formal receipt for you, Major. We must now resume our journey. Until we meet again. *Dewa mata.*"

"*Shitsurei itashimasu kakka.* May I have permission to leave, Excellency?"

He saluted, and Henderson saluted back. I nodded to Buisman, who came forward and slid the port window shut. The Major stepped back, again saluted and strode back to his truck.

"Proceed to take off at once," I called to Coe.

"Very good, sir." He called up the control tower. "Request clearance for priority take-off for General Yamaji's plane. Thank you. Goodbye."

He ran up each engine in turn, checking the gauges carefully, then both together, and released the brakes. With half our fuel gone we bucketed along and the tail came up readily; then the take-off was easy and we were airborne. Major Hashimoto was still standing there. What thoughts were going through his head? I felt a pang of sympathy for him when the deception was eventually discovered.

Below us were buffalo carts laden with rice, and dusty villages with the occasional golden pagoda set with minute twinkling mirrors that heliogaphed the sun back to us.

'No relaxing for ten minutes' had been the order, and we continued to scan the ground and sky all around. We climbed steadily, turning in the general direction of Bangkok for the benefit of any observer. Then we were safely up in the clouds.

Henderson said at last, "I really think we've pulled it off."

There was no wild rejoicing. We could still hardly believe it – and there was still the long trek home. The intensity of those ten minutes at Mingaladon still dominated our thoughts, and still intermittently dominates mine to this day. As I heard a child say, much later: "Once upon a time, nothing happened." That was more than we had dared to hope for.

Now that we were hidden from the ground we could swing north. We kept climbing bumpily, hoping to turn west about 25,000 feet so as to get safely out to sea. As we broke through the cloud sheet we saw that route blocked by a typical monsoon pattern: towering grey-blue cumulonimbus masses, some already turning black.

Burma monsoon weather produces some of the most dangerous flying conditions in the world. Turbulence can wrench a plane out of the pilot's control, or turn it round without his knowing. Electrical storms can put his compass out of action. One fighter squadron lost half its number from flying into cloud and breaking up. Many mountains run up to 10,000 feet, so it's not safe to fly underneath. The only chance is to fly above the cloud – but not when it reaches 60,000 feet or more, twice the aircraft's ceiling.

The ride became rougher and rain burst in clattering showers as we lurched in the crosswinds. Buisman went forward to help plot our best course. Westwards was ruled out by the monsoon clouds.

Southwards meant returning to Mingaladon; we might run out of fuel, and by now our visit might have stirred up a hornets' nest. Eastwards merely postponed the decision; every mile took us away from our base. Northwards was the only possibility, in the hope of eventually breaking out westwards.

The pilots had left their intercom on and were arguing. Coe wanted to skirt the clouds and get out to sea quickly.

"The theory's fine, buster, but you haven't flown in monsoon clouds and I have."

"If you keep north of the black centre I'll bet you'll find calmer weather."

"That's true too, but you know what's inside the cloud?"

"Go on."

"Mountain peaks. Old friends. I've a great respect for them."

"Can't you go clear over them?"

"In calm weather, yes. In this stuff, the downdraught makes it a damn sight too risky."

"What about going under the storm?"

"There's no underneath. The storm reaches right down to the foothills. Look, for heaven's sake, stop beefing. I know this country too bloody well for comfort. I don't scare easily, *but I am not flying through that lot.* We are going up to our ceiling and flying north up the Irrawaddy valley and that's that."

Coe muttered something tetchily. "Oh shuddup," exploded Taylor. Was it only a week ago that we had joked about plots in which the pilots quarrelled while they were over the target? Now, with the target behind us, the dangers ahead still threatened us.

This nightmarish journey seemed to last for ever. At one point we could make out a stretch of river flowing south-west between sandbanks. Taylor was sure that it was the Irrawaddy near Mandalay. If he was right we were almost due east of Cox's Bazaar, but dared not approach because Mount Victoria, of 10,000 feet, stood between. North-west and north the inaccessible ranges rose higher still.

"Damnation," said Taylor. "I backed the wrong horse. Perhaps Coe was right. We'll have to go south-west in case there's a gap in the clouds nearer the coast. I've known that happen."

Buisman took over the controls while Taylor and Coe relaxed. They had been flying for four hours in atrocious conditions, and concentration can last just so far and no further. We were about to cross the main Arakan range.

I'll spare you the details of the next hour. All three experienced fliers agreed that it was the worst flight they had known. Flying blind for long periods is always demoralising, but when the plane is being wrenched bodily in every direction in turn, and the engines are labouring with changing air currents all the time, it becomes hellish. At the height of the storm Coe said that the oil pressure in the starboard engine was fluctuating, but the plane seemed intact otherwise.

"There's one piece of good news," Taylor told us. "I've found that missing chart. It was folded inside a bigger sheet. I hope Preston's so chuffed when we get back that he'll forget about my losing it."

After an hour the worst was over and we knew we must be near the coast. The question was: where? The chain of airfields down the coast made the answer urgent. As the cloud thinned we studied the tangle of creeks and islands below and tried to match them to the maps. Buisman got there first.

"Climb quick as you can. We are nearly over Cheduba airfield. Fly north-west."

Cheduba! We were much too far south. Would the fuel last? How soon was it safe to use our radio to ask for an escort? Had the Japs spotted us? If so, only our markings could save us, assuming they saw them in time. Any unexpected aircraft was likely to be fair game.

Coe's voice on the intercom: "Let's hope Cheduba hasn't recovered from the RAF raid. We are about 250 miles south of Cox's Bazaar. We are turning north and that means one and a half hours' flying at this speed. We want to throttle down to save fuel and take the strain off that starboard engine. It's overheating and the oil pressure is acting crazy."

"Do that," Henderson agreed. "Call up CB, Buisman, and send 7272 plus our probable position in cipher."

Buisman got busy and then announced, "They've scrambled three Spitfires and more will follow. They're being refuelled after the last sortie."

We were only 100 miles from the Jap-held coast, and closing on it. We couldn't afford the fuel to detour away from their nearby airfield at Akyab, and Cox's Bazaar, at our reduced speed, must be nearly two hours away. It was a gamble, especially as we had a suspect engine.

"How bad is it?" Henderson asked.

"You never know. Throttling it down will help, but the gauge could be exaggerating. It could last out an hour or more, or it could pack up any moment. We dare not risk flying on one engine before we have to, especially with Japs around. At least we're saving fuel, which is our other headache."

"OK, keep nursing it. We'll have to get our friends to help. Get me CB on the radio-telephone."

With them he was as crisp as he dared to be, remembering that he had stopped being a General, even an enemy General, and was back to being a mere British Army Major bargaining with the RAF.

"Look, we've done the job. Can't you get a move on and send more aircraft in case we have to ditch? I don't care where you get them from."

I couldn't hear the reply but I saw his frown deepen and his language became more picturesque, the accent more 'Loch Leven', as he called it.

"For Pete's sake, I don't know who I'm speaking to, but however senior you are I give you fair warning. Ring your AOC, tell him that Operation Paperchase went perfectly and we've got the goods. What's that? I don't care if *you* don't understand. I assure you *he* will. Tell him how we are placed. If you don't pull out all the stops to help us he'll put the skids under you so fast you'll never touch ground again."

That concluded the conversation. Soon afterwards the three Spitfires arrived, waggled their wings to show they knew about us, and took up station: one on each side, one astern and above us. Buisman established radio contact with them and we breathed more freely.

The starboard engine sounded unhappy. We had covered another fifty-five miles and kept the same height of 25,000 feet. Taylor checked his sums: 150 miles to go to CB – an hour's flight – and only eighty-five miles from the Jap airfield at Ramree. The radio crackled again. One of the Spitfires said that Jap fighters were reported to be scrambling at Akyab and they were going to take them on. They left in a hurry climbing steeply so as to have the advantage of height and the sun behind them. Buisman checked his cannon by firing a short burst. Henderson and I tried to recall the drill for firing at fighters.

We saw the Japanese, six Zeros. The frustrating thing was that our plane in proper working order could fly almost as fast as theirs, but we were hobbling along on one leg with no reserve power for manoeuvring. They split up into two groups of three and prepared to attack.

The first was halfway down towards us when a Spitfire caught up with him, and immediately his heavy armament sent bits flying off the Zero. Henderson fired a short burst but saw no hits. Then cannon-shell started hammering into our fuselage before the second Zero was similarly jumped on. The third perhaps saw what happened to the first two, and lost his concentration when he spotted the third Spitfire on his tail. At any event he broke off his attack. Had he seen our markings? No – he was preparing to come in again.

I never saw the fourth, but there was a terrific din from the turret above us. Buisman fired the 20-mm cannon and gave a yell, and the Zero dived past in a trail of smoke, leaving rows of bullet holes in our port wing and along the fuselage. Had they hit anything vital?

That left three Zeros: Number three who had now climbed above us again, and numbers five and six who had not yet attacked. At that point Coe must have found their radio frequency; he was furiously bellowing in Japanese, "You idiots, you are attacking a Japanese general's plane from Imperial HQ. Do you want to be court-martialled? Leave us alone and go for those accursed Spitfires."

That kept them at bay while they decided what to do next. Were they wondering why the Spitfires had not attacked us? The logic was too tangled to help them or us. At that moment, thank God, more Spitfires arrived and the Zeros made for home, the centre of an almighty dogfight.

Buisman called from his turret, "Can you please help? I think I stopped a bullet."

We scrambled up. He had turned back the bottom of one leg of his flying breeches and was holding a handkerchief against his calf. Henderson looked at it carefully and whistled. "A lucky shot for you, Piet. You didn't stop it. It went right through the fleshy part and came out the other side." I identified the Japanese antiseptic cream and he set to work.

Now we had to take stock again. Bullets had hit the cockpit, missing both pilots but smashing the altimeter dial. We should need the escort to give us a running commentary on our height when we landed. Other shots had riddled the transparent canopy, and there was another cluster of holes further back. The starboard engine had got no worse; the pilots had ignored the fight and concentrated on cosseting it. We had lost some height but were still at about 15,000. Fuel was very low and we still had 100 miles to go.

"I'd like to weaken the mixture to save fuel," Coe said, "but we could harm the engine. I dare not do it. Will someone please look at the elevators? The other controls are OK." He sounded puzzled rather than alarmed. Henderson and I looked out of the side blisters but could see nothing wrong.

"The plane doesn't respond at all."

Buisman had been checking along each side of the fuselage. "No surprise. That last shooting has broken some control wires. Is there any spare wire?"

Apparently not. Then he remembered the chain that held the opened hatch off the ground. We wrenched it loose, and by bending the broken ends of wire we formed a temporary link which would hold if handled gently. I told Coe what we'd done. "Sounds like Rube Goldberg to me."

"We call him Heath Robinson," I said.

Cox's Bazaar told us that several coastal craft were stationed along our route in case we had to ditch. We had life rafts and dinghy packs; we simply needed to stay up as long as we could.

Henderson remembered the codebook. Buisman grinned. "Mae West can carry it."

The Mae West was the airman's inflatable life jacket. We fastened the pair of books in a bulky waterproof jacket and he stowed it in his Mae West because he was, he claimed, a strong swimmer even with a stiff leg. We found things to throw out to lighten the load: our personal guns and grenades, and the oxygen bottles now that we were down to 10,000 feet.

Seventy miles to go, losing height all the time. The coast was visible in the setting sun and the sea was shallower and paler, shelving into wide sands which ran back to the promontory on which Cox's Bazaar sprawls.

Forty miles and down to 8,000. I could see the vessels as tiny glowing specks. Buisman stood up to test his leg and there was a metallic tinkle on the floor. It was the bullet, which had flattened itself against a strut, so he kept it as a memento.

The bad engine was beginning to splutter and oily smoke was drifting out. Coe had feathered that airscrew so that it wouldn't exert a braking effect on that side. He called up CB to check the wind direction.

"Sorry, it's still south-west, right behind you, light to fresh. You'll have to come in south of here, keep banking to port and run straight in. There's a fine array of crash tenders, fire engines and ambulances standing by."

Taylor took over the radio. "You've got one detail wrong. It's our starboard engine that's conking out. I'll have to come in low over the island and keep turning to starboard. I'll hit the deck as gently as I can. Hang on, I've just had a thought. I had a crash landing last month with one dud engine. It put such a strain on the undercart that one leg collapsed. There was a hellish great shower of sparks and the whole plane caught fire. I got out just in time. Not again. I'll do a belly-landing, wheels up, on the sand at the edge of the airfield. We'll come in over the creek, let down gently over the damp part, and slither to somewhere near the end of the main runway. Got all that? Brief those fire-trucks. If I write it off at least it's not our tax-payers' money."

Twenty miles, 3,000 feet; about eight minutes to go. The scheme made good sense. Taylor said he had practised golf shots along that sandy shore while he was stationed at CB and had a fair mental picture of the contours.

Ten miles, 1,500 feet; four minutes. Losing height and speed meant some delicate balancing of factors. If we arrived too low, too soon, we had no controllable power to lift us again. If we stayed too high, too long, we should have to descend more steeply and that would push our landing speed up dangerously. We had no power to make a second attempt. We had to find exactly the angle to bring us to the right part of the sandbanks at the right height and speed. That sort of calculation could be arrived at only by skill, cool nerves and a lot of experience in tight corners.

"Flaps right down, but don't put the undercart down from force of habit. Remember we're doing a belly-flop."

Five miles, 900 feet. A couple of minutes more. Taylor was taking us wide to the north of Maiskhal Island, which lies just north-west of the airfield with a shallow inlet between. The sun silhouetted the sandbanks against a purple background of meandering channels. The plane's distorted shadow flickered across the tawny mudflats beyond.

Coe was juggling with the starboard engine controls all the time; occasionally it produced some noise and power and eased the strain on the controls. As we cautiously banked to starboard we lost more height by side-slipping, creeping down to 700, 500, then 350 feet. Still too high and a shade too fast, so he throttled the good engine down low and by a careful zigzag got down to 200, 100, 50 feet.

The sand ahead was featureless but there was plenty of it. Coe kept calling out his estimate of our height as seen through his side window. Taylor lost more height by fishtailing the rudder while holding the plane level and keeping it in the air as long as possible. He throttled both engines right back and we floated a few yards above the brackish water of the little creek. On the far side the sand rose gently and we touched, slid and bumped along it for several hundred yards.

I saw a crash tender, an ambulance and a fire engine racing towards us, throwing up haloes of sand. We slithered to a halt. Dead silence inside. Nothing caught fire. The yielding sand had cushioned the underside of the fuselage and it would need little more than a repaint. Only the two airscrews were wrecked, their tips bent back as they bit into the sand.

"*Banzai* – hooray," shouted Henderson.

POSTSCRIPT

What happened afterwards?

The rescue gang arrived, broke open the side blisters and helped us down ladders. They were torn between congratulating us on the landing and arresting us as enemy airmen, so we were glad to see Preston and Lewis close behind. For once Preston seemed lost for words, but at last he got out, "Congratulations, the lot of you. Did you get it?"

Our prize, the small parcel that was the cause of the whole operation, was still in Buisman's Mae West and we had forgotten about it. We had the pleasure of putting it in Preston's hands.

The pleasure didn't last long. Just then Coe wormed his way back through the fuselage: "Get the medics, quick. Taylor has passed out. I can't rouse him at all." The MO's verdict was immediate: some sort of heart attack. The post-mortem would give the details. He must have died just as he relaxed after pulling off that miraculous landing. They told us later that the fuel would have lasted barely five minutes more.

We stayed at Cox's Bazaar that night and Preston did recite 'The green eye of the little yellow God', to celebrate. Buisman spent an hour in the sick bay having his bullet wound treated and it healed fast, especially after we flew to the fresh air of Ranchi next morning. I quickly got rid of the malaria. We stayed there until Sen Gupta, Srivastava, pumice and soap had removed most of the dye.

Taylor was buried in the cemetery beside Ranchi church. His unofficial epitaph? He had often been the odd man out – the buccaneer: bossy, moody, careless over details that might have blown the whole operation sky-high. Yet he could be a good friend, the flight plan was his creation, and that extraordinary last landing had been a triumph.

Hira Lal? We never found out what happened to him. There was no evidence of a leak, and we now knew that he hadn't taken Taylor's chart. We had to presume that the timing of the Japanese raid on Cox's Bazaar was sheer coincidence. "But it put the fear of God into me," Preston said. "You see why I had to warn you."

The codebook? You may find this hard to believe but I cannot remember if they changed to the new book or not. I don't think they did. Yet that suggests that they rumbled us. How? Only by learning that Hashimoto handed it over. But then our bogus signal, which tricked him into it, showed that the old book too was compromised. If he hushed up the incident, knowing that Tokyo would go berserk once they knew, then why didn't they change books as planned? The argument goes round in a circle.

Try it the other way round. If I'm wrong and they did change books, Hashimoto would have been in the soup. Without his copy Rangoon couldn't decode incoming signals or encode their own. Every other signals unit in the network would complain. He couldn't hope to keep it secret; a court-martial would follow. Knowing that, might he have arranged his own Paperchase and stolen the copy from his old HQ at Prome? It gets more fanciful all the time.

Perhaps the answer lies in the way the war was going against Japan just then. Even if they realised that *both* books were compromised, they probably had no reserve book ready. Even if they had, it would take an age to distribute. They had more pressing things to worry about.

But this is all speculation. It made no odds to us. We had both books, one broken, one stolen, and we continued to read 2244 traffic as before.

It soon showed, much as the General had supposed, that Kimura expected our main attack to be aimed at Mandalay itself and planned his defences south of the Irrawaddy. The General's plan was ingenious and deceived Kimura. In order to sustain Kimura's belief – the old legend says, 'He who holds Mandalay holds Burma' – he dispatched 33 Corps in a direct assault on it. But he also sent 4 Corps in his promised right hook down remote valleys far to the west, in complete secrecy and with some subtle feints to distract attention from it. It was then to cross the Irrawaddy well away from Mandalay and use an armoured column – a novelty in that area – to race across and seize the vital town and airfields of Meiktila, seventy-five miles south of Mandalay and right athwart its communications.

That clinched the matter. Though there was still stiff fighting ahead, the Japanese in Burma were decisively broken. As he pushed towards Rangoon their resistance, though hardly less fanatical, grew steadily more disorganised. In the end the question was which of our divisions would reach Rangoon first. In fact, the long-awaited amphibious assault, Operation Dracula, beat them both by a few hours. The city fell as the monsoon rains broke. That was in early May 1945, three months before Hiroshima.

It took almost eighteen months after the Japanese capitulation in August 1945 for the last of us to get home. The prisoners of war had to be first in the queue for scarce ships and aircraft before anyone could start ferrying the tens of thousands of troops back to Europe. Anyway, the fighting didn't stop at once. Even after Tokyo's surrender, some local Japanese commanders refused to comply with their Emperor's order to lay down their arms. They could not believe it. In Burma, pairs of British and Japanese officers had to go forward under a white flag to convince them that the war was over, and my signals colleagues surprised their enemy counterparts by openly intervening on their networks to pass the surrender message on to them.

In Malaya the planned invasion across the beaches, Operation Zipper, still went ahead weeks after the surrender, and eventually succeeded despite a planning fiasco. In the East Indies the Indonesians saw their chance 'after three and a half centuries of Dutch occupation and three and a half years of Japanese oppression' to declare themselves independent. The same happened in Indo-China.

The members of our team dispersed and were caught up in this delay and confusion. Wallace was badly injured when his group ran into an ambush prepared by a rival Chinese gang for their common enemy. His right leg was broken in two places by a hand grenade, and although it was cleverly operated on in a jungle hospital, he still limps. He spent some time with his parents in England before returning to Malaya to work in his old area of Pahang. Later he played an important part in establishing the first Malayan National Park. Lee was reunited with his parents, who had somehow survived the occupation of Singapore, and later he took over his father's business. He now runs the main Pentax agency there, and he and Wallace recently collaborated in producing the first volume of *Malayan Butterflies in Colour*, of which they kindly sent a copy to each of us.

Buisman found his wife and daughters emaciated but otherwise well. They moved up to the healthier climate of Bandung, where he was born. He has an office job there with his old oil company, but still finds excuses for flying round that beautiful country. Sometimes he goes further afield, and recently he arranged a meeting with Wallace and Lee in Singapore. Coe, like Lee, took charge of the family business when his father retired, but spends most of his energies in selling light aircraft to millionaires, whose ranks he looks likely to join soon.

I went back to Cambridge to finish my degree course, married, and after several overseas jobs returned there to lecture in music. Henderson never quite remarried. He moved to a lectureship at The Other Place and is an authority on the German poet and novelist, Novalis; his book, *The Blue Flower*, on this optimistic but unfortunate man, has been widely praised. We have both kept our Japanese identity cards as souvenirs. Lewis returned to teaching and became head of a flourishing school in north Wales. His poems and his articles on poetry frequently appear in various literary journals.

Preston retired from the Army a few years later, after some unusual assignments which there is no room to describe here, and immediately dropped the 'Colonel', to the indignation of his colleagues. I saw a good deal of him when as plain Anthony Preston he later came up to Cambridge as an adult student, exploring in turn Oriental languages, philosophy and medieval history, never caring in the least about examination results. Soon after the war he had married Helen, the same girl who had arranged Wallace's flight from Ceylon at the start of his mission. They are among the happiest and most open-minded people I know. They have a welcoming house near Wendover and a Burmese cat called Maymyo. Preston once gave away the prizes at Lewis's school, and I gather that this was a memorable and hilarious performance. He has also been called in, from time to time, to help with delicate odd jobs when ordinary police or intelligence work was ruled out.

We exchange Christmas cards and several of us have met, accidentally or deliberately, from time to time. We have never reassembled as a complete group. It doesn't seem to matter. None of us is very keen on looking backwards.

So why, you may very well ask, why write this book about the past?

The answer is, I think, that it has haunted me long enough. Telling the story may help me to forget it.

Appendix:
Codes And Codebreaking

In case you are interested in the intricacies of the 2244 code sys-tem, used by the Japanese Army Air Force, this is how I tried to explain it to the team at Ranchi:

1. CODEBOOK (see page 170)

In two parts, each containing 10,000 four-digit code-groups. The first was used for *sending and encoding* messages, and was arranged in the Japanese equivalent of alphabetical order – the traditional order of 'radicals' or basic elements in the characters. Each group stood for a word, phrase, numeral and so on, and the groups were assigned in random order to help security. This book was very much like a telephone directory in format.

The other book was for *receiving and decoding* messages, resem-bling the list that a telephone company consults to see who rents a particular number. Here the same code-groups were arranged in numerical order from 0000 to 9999.

The time-honoured way to use this was simply to write out your mes-sage in clear, and encode it by finding the right groups one by one – very much like using a dictionary. If you sent out many messages like this, the enemy would quickly break them on the basis of frequency, context and probability. So the Japs added two more layers for further security.

2. NUMERICAL KEY

A book of 100 pages, each containing 100 random four-digit groups arranged in ten columns and ten rows.

3. SUBSTITUTION TABLE

A small square containing 100 digits randomly arranged in ten columns and ten rows.

4. PROCEDURE

"Suppose you are in command of a Japanese Army Air Force station in Burma which was raided yesterday by the RAF." (Taylor, who had been looking bored, came to life.) "You draft a message beginning: 'On October 6th enemy bombers attacked our ground installations and aircraft which were being refuelled.' Your cipher clerk picks up the 2244 Book One, a typical page of which looks like this."* (A list of various units and headquarters, interesting to us because 9424 in the second column is Kôkû Tokushu Tsushintai or Air Special Communications Unit – our opposite numbers who tried to intercept and break our signals.) "He looks up each word of your text in turn and writes down the code-group for it: *ju-gatsu* (October – literally 10th month) is 2671; *roku-hi* (6th) is 8453; *teki* (enemy) is 6967; *bakugeki-ki* (bombers) is 5129; *wa* (indicates subject of verb) is 0813; and so on, giving the code-text 2671 8453 6967 5129 0813 etc.

"Now he picks up the *keybook*," (see Section 2) "opens it at random, shuts his eyes and selects a random starting point. If that is on page 16, column 3, row 7, he writes down the indicator 1637 at the head of the text. Without that his colleague who receives and decrypts the signal will be lost. Next he writes out one key-group, starting at that point, under every group of the code-text, continuing to the end of the message."

2671 8453 6967 5129 0813 etc. (code-text)

(1637) 9814 5205 7348 3682 4987 etc. (key-text).

"I know," exclaimed Preston triumphantly. "You add the two lines together and transmit the result."

181

"Hopelessly out of date. That worked until the 1930s or so. By the 1940s that was seen – at least by the Japanese, and I hope by us – as much too easy to break. Instead you get your substitution table" (see Section 3) "like this:"

	0	1	2	3	4	5	6	7	8	9
0	4	7	3	0	5	9	2	6	1	8
1	9	5	1	8	3	0	6	2	7	4
2	5	0	7	4	2	1	8	6	9	3
3	3	9	2	7	4	6	0	1	8	5
4	2	3	8	0	9	7	0	4	1	5
5	7	2	0	1	3	5	9	8	4	6
6	0	1	9	3	8	4	7	6	5	2
7	1	8	6	4	2	7	5	0	9	3
8	6	1	9	5	7	2	3	8	0	4
9	8	4	7	2	6	3	1	5	7	0

"Then use the two lines to make a third: take each pair of upper and lower figures in turn, disregarding the indicator 1637. Use the first figure of the top line to give the column of the square, and the first figure of the second line to give the row, and write down the figure where they cross to give the signal text.

2671 8453 6967 5129 0813 etc (columns)
9814 5205 7348 3682 4987 etc (rows)
(1637) 7323 4291 5508 6193 2714 etc (signal text)"

"Sometimes they put the discriminant 2244 before the 1637, etc., to show which system they're using."

"You say you chaps can still break this stuff?" asked Preston.

"Oh yes, given enough signals traffic. The hardest thing is breaking into it starting from scratch, and of course all their material is regularly changed. But the Japs are bound to use radio signals a lot. The telephone system isn't up to much, and the cable and telex hardly exist in Burma, so there are plenty of signals for us to work on. The best thing is if they start re-using material that they've used before because they've got nothing else in reserve.

"There was a rumour at Bletchley Park, where I learnt the trade, that one of the Germans who had the job of inventing new random material all the time for Enigma – ring-settings, plugboard-settings, wheel-orders and so forth – must have got bored, said, 'To hell with it,' and started re-using old ones."

"Did we find out?"

"Would I be telling you, if we hadn't?"

My book *Codebreaker in the Far East* (Cass 1989 and Oxford 1995) and my joint book with Sir Harry Hinsley, *Codebreakers: the Inside Story of Bletchley Park* (Oxford 1993 and 1994), give fuller accounts of the whole subject. A.S.

CODEBOOK

4906	
6430	飛脚
0258	
6240	航
8351	
4770	航空
3935	航空路部
4182	航空路部司令部
7036	航空IC
0544	
3973	航空教育隊
3782	航空地區司令部
0700	航空特殊無線隊
4698	航空特殊情報隊
9424	航空特殊通信隊
0670	航空通信司令部
3755	航空通信團
6829	
7050	航空通信連隊

Printed by Amazon Italia Logistica S.r.l.
Torrazza Piemonte (TO), Italy

13889905R00117